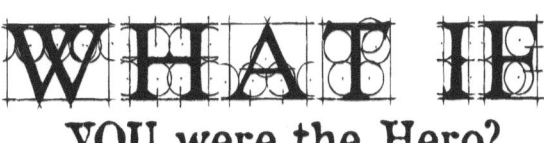

WHAT IF

...YOU were the Hero?

A Wanted Hero series

by
Jaime Buckley

CROSS POINT
WHAT IF...YOU were the Hero? #1

For more information, please visit wantedhero.com

Published by On The Fly Publications

This is a work of fiction. Names, characters, places, brands, media, and incidents are either the product of the author's imagination or are used fictitiously.

First Publishing: 2014
Printed in the USA

ISBN# 978-1-61463-052-4

Cover Design & Illustrations by Jaime D. Buckley
Page Arrangements & Editing by Nathan Taylor
Author Photograph by Kelly Cannon Photography

WANTED HERO BOOKS

Chronicles of a Hero

- Prelude to a Hero #0.5 -
- Race to Til-Thorin #1 -
- Trench Wars #2 -
- The Truth About Lies #3 -

Höbin Luckyfeller's Fieldguide

- Demoni Vankil -
- Bloodsticks -

Letters to Alhannah

- How I Met Your Mother -

WANTED HERO GAMES

- Race to Til-Thorin card game -
- Bloodsticks -
- G.E.A.R.S. -
- Go SMILEY! -

WARNING!!!!

Do not read this book straight through from beginning to end...that's exactly what MAHAN wants! To prevent you from becoming yet another hero to oppose him...

These pages contain many secrets for you to discover--new challenges to face and multiple endings to experience.

It all depends upon your CHOICE.

You are responsible for the results, because you direct the story with each and every choice you make. When you make a choice, follow the instructions to see what happens next.

Remember--you cannot go back! Think carefully and choose wisely before making a move! The wrong choice can be your last..while the right choice can affect the future of world forever!!

GOOD LUCK

The World Right Now

You have heard rumors.

The shadows of evil are growing across the sea and have already touched your lands. The Lord of Darkness is waging open war upon the world of mortals. Gathering his armies from the foul places of the world, he seeks to divide and conquer the races of light.

The year is 6013s (sundering).

Dark armies have invaded every nation but that of the Nocturi, who shroud their island in magic. The Kutollum have successfully defended their mountain homelands of ice and stone, temporarily driving the hordes back into the frozen sea. The Evolu, after a season of bitter war and death, have been forced to flee their homelands, to save what is left of their people. The powerful Getti, who usually live in secret, feel the rising tempest upon the land. As nature groans, they have come forth in aid...and record sightings have been made of the gentle giants within the populated cities and sea ports of the world. Even the gnomes, the smallest and weakest of all, have sent those with hearts so full of righteous indignation, to use their forbidden magic in defense of the land.

You have a decision to make. Those you know and those you care about are already suffering because of the wars that are encroaching upon them. Unless the evil is stopped, they will perish. Your homeland will die.

High King Gaston has sent a proclamation to every able-bodied citizen—calling all patriots to the human capital of Andilain. The nation is gathering and the great armies of the world have answered the call, uniting under one banner. There is soon to be a *Gathering of Kings*.

The greatest alliance in history is about to be formed.

Introduction

You are traveling with your two closest friends: Dorbane, a stout, grumpy, yet loyal Kutollum warrior...and Valda, a beautiful young Gypsy girl. You have been traveling for weeks towards the capital city of Andilain, across mountain and plain. It's been a long trek, pushing through the Tilliman Highlands, around the mountain of Idumea and through the fields of Ashbrook and Fallcreek. You're in good company. You laugh, sing and talk about your plans. The future is before you as decorated, respected and soon-to-be-famous members of the Kings Army. That's the plan, anyway.

The trip is nearly over. By sunset tomorrow, you will be enlisting in the greatest military force this world has ever seen.

The season is fading, and the nights are growing longer. As the sun starts to set upon the green hills of the land, you notice that travelers upon the roads quickly become scarce. Most refuse to travel during the night. It's not uncommon to hear rumors of evil things lurking in the shadows of the forest. Some whisper of monsters. Those wiser whisper of invaders and the awakening of darker magic.

"Can't we rest?" complains Valda out loud, "We've been walking all day and my feet are killing me!"

Her raven black hair reflects the last rays of sunlight, shimmering over slender, tan shoulders. She gives you a pleading look that you always find hard to resist. When this fails to get the desired sympathy, she bats her eyes at you.

Dorbane chuckles, "Oh give the girl a break...it's not going to hurt our progress and she'll finally stop complaining!"

You laugh. "Alright. We take a break for a half-hour, but then we push on through the night. I want to be in Andilain by morning light, agreed?"

"Agreed!" she squeals and bounces over to Dorbane to give the Kutollum a kiss on the cheek.

You can't help but grin. The three of you have always been close. At least as long as you can remember, anyway...ever since the raids on your village of Sangil. Both you and Valda were orphans to begin with, but when the Kutollum assisted the humans in fighting off attacks from the Southern Shores, Dorbane found himself without a father. The campaign was long and bloody. Few survived the ravaging assaults as the enemy pushed inland. It was within the mountains that the battle turned and was finally won—with the help of the citizens. Regular men and women, fighting for survival...and who came to the aid of the army.

In the final conflict, Dorbane had lost his father.

When the soldiers moved on, he decided to stay with a young human who had saved his life.

That human is *you.*

The Gypsy girl finds a log stump, sits down, pulls off her soft leather boots and shakes out the gravel. "I hate walking this far," she mumbles with a huff. "And I *told* you we should have brought more bread! I'm starving."

Dorbane chuckles, "I thought you Gypsies loved to wander—that it's in your *blood*?"

"Wander...not march like a stone dwarf," she corrects him. She looks up at you with a sweet expression on her face. "I'm sorry. You know I'd follow you anywhere." She pauses and gives you a comical smirk, "Just wish I knew where anywhere *was.*"

You laugh together.

Arrival

Just as the last light wanes on the horizon, you reach Cross Point, the main intersection of the kings highway. It's where the merchant paths of the north, south, east and west meet together. The guard post is empty—a small house made of stone and a thatch roof. The door is open, the roads now deserted.

The last travelers have already moved on.

You hear the whistling of a sailors tune...and a wagon slowly rolls up the road. The giant wooden wheels make their thump-thump-thumping sound over gravel and holes in the road. You step aside to let it pass. The wagon is loaded with large barrels. An old man, hunched over in his seat, nods to each of you as he rolls by. His long, thin white beard sways in the night wind as he calls out, though not looking back.

"Better be getting along, young ones...not a good idea to be out in the forest after dark!"

He stops at the crossing and pulls a bucket from under the seat. With a grunt and a complaint or two under his breath, he dismounts the wagon in an awkward and comical fashion. You all watch as he stiffly shuffles around to his shipment of containers and fills the bucket with oil from the barrels. One by one he replenishes the lanterns under the road-sign, pointing north. A sign which says: Castle Andilain.

The old man continues to whistle to himself as he works lighting the lantern.

"Look at that," whispers Dorbane, nudging you. He squints, his keen Kutollum eyes peering through the dim light. "There, in the trees to the west!" He nudges you again, insistent.

You and Valda have difficulty at first, but sure enough—you're able to make out the outline of a man moving along the distant tree line.

He seems to be...dragging a body down the embankment and into the forest!

"Is...that a guard?" you ask out loud.

Valda's hand goes to the gem encrusted knife at her hip. She scans the rest of the trees around you warily. "It would explain why the guard post is empty."

With the lantern lit, the old man drops the bucket into the back of his wagon and pulls himself back into his seat. He's completely oblivious to the movements just over his shoulder. Without a word, he clicks his tongue and the animal walks on. Within minutes, the wagon...and the sound of the old man's whistling, are gone.

Dorbane looks at you soberly. "What now?"

- If you decide to investigate the suspicious soldier, go to page 59.
- If you decide to hurry on and make Castle Andilain before dawn, go to page 8.

8. Hurry On To Castle Andilain

"We're here to serve this country," you give your friends a stern look, "and I don't know about you—but the sooner we get to an Inn, the better."

Dorbane sighs, then rubs his neck, "Right. I am beat." He rolls his eyes at the Gypsy, smirking, "...and I'd like her to stop complaining."

"Hey!" Valda squeaks, "Toadstool," and jabs the Kutollum in the shoulder. "I agree, though," she adds, "Let's get to warm beds and full bellies as quickly as possible."

Nodding, you lead your friends up the Kings Highway in the direction the old man left.

The moons give their light, casting a blue and red tinted glow to the road. You take several breaks through the night, but as the sun begins to rise, you see the peaks of the famed Castle Andilain.

"Wow," Valda gasps. The sunlight cuts through the sky and streaks across the landscape, shimmering off the white stone of the castle walls. The stronghold almost looks like sculptured pearl. The blue and red banners can be seen draped from the highest towers. She smiles. "We're finally going to be a part of something great."

Dorbane looks at you and smirks. "Humans, hah! You're so easily impressed."

You roll your eyes.

The Kutollum slaps you on the back, "Try crafting an entire city from the innards of a live volcano, nestled in the frozen wastelands of the North, where the landscape glitters like diamonds...then tell me this is impressive."

"You just had to ruin my moment, didn't you?" Valda grumbles, marching down the road.

Dorbane looks at you with feigned innocence, "What did I do?"

- If you decide to enlist right away, go to page 106.
- If you want to have a drink and get some food at the local Inn first, go to page 62.

10. Find Friends

Keeping to the shadows, you move in a wide arc, staying far from the firelight. The last thing you want is to be discovered. As you approach the edge of the campsite, you discover Valda crouched behind a fallen tree. She motions for you to stay low and holds a finger to her lips.

There's no sign of Dorbane.

From your vantage point, you can see the clearing—the whole area revealed by the campfire. Four bodies lie against the far embankment, a gentle slope with thick trees growing higher up the incline. You notice each with a sac over their head, hands tied behind their backs.

"Prisoners?" you whisper.

"One of them's a woman," Valda hisses.

"How can you tell?"

She jabs a finger at the last figure. Sure enough, you then notice the smallest body is wearing a dress.

Closer to both of you, sitting next to the fire, is a soldier. His helm reflects the dancing flames of the firelight. Two others stand near the bodies—also soldiers. They look to be arguing, but you can't hear what they're saying. All three are wearing the blue and red tabard of Andilain.

With an abrupt plop, Dorbane falls down between you and Valda. He's breathing hard.

"I worked my way around the forest," he huffs, trying to stay quiet, "Wanted to make sure no one could sneak up on us."

"And?" you ask.

"...and they're alone," grins the Kutollum. But his expression turns grave, "They're also talking about killing the three prisoners."

"There's four prisoners," you correct him.

"No," Dorbane shakes his head, then points to the shortest of the bodies. "They have three humans and a Kutollum. They mean to frame the deaths on the dwarf."

Your fondness for the North People is deep. You growl from your chest, "Not good."

One of the standing soldiers draws a long knife...and starts walking towards the bodies.

- If you decide to rush the soldiers, go to page 56.
- Make animal sounds to draw them away, go to page 89.

12. Toma

As you round the bend, the scene has already unfolded.

There are two men, fully shrouded under their hoods, barring the path of the captains. Both strangers are brandishing long knives—their polished blades reflecting the starlight. On the ground before them is a man, bound and gagged. A sack over his head hides his features. He tries to struggle, but the larger of the two captors yanks on the rope of the sack—restricting his airflow.

The other captor kicks the bound man in the back. The wiry body falls forward and stops moving.

"What is this?" demands Deron. He reaches for his sword, but a knife at his throat stops him.

"Do it!" hisses Toma, looking to the two looming figures, "Slit the elf's throat!"

"What!??" gasps Deron, "Toma...why would you..."

His laughter is uncontrollable. Triumphant. Toma strikes the Kutollum across the jaw, knocking Deron to the ground.

"You...*pig!* There's no one that hates your filthy breed more than I. You don't belong in Andilain! You and these tree hugging elves have been a plague to this land since you arrived!!"

With a swift kick, Toma sends the captain rolling in the dirt.

"What better way to get rid of both your filthy races, than to murder Lord Raywhen's son..." he leans down to the dwarf, "...and frame you for it!"

Spinning back to the two hooded men, "Did you hear me, you morons!? Slit that elf-bastards throat!"

As the last word leaves his lips, the alley is flooded with soldiers.

The Royal Guard of Andilain.

Torches held high, the polished armor of High King Gaston's elite surrounds the two hooded figures.

"Toma Thornberry," grins Marshall Golace, taking a puff on his pipe, "You are under arrest on charges of kidnapping, attempted murder and sedition."

Rising from the ground, Captain Deron leans close to the Marshall. "May I?"

The Marshall gives Toma a sideways glance. Golace turns his back...and in perfect, obedient unison, his men do the same.

The heavy leather glove is all that softens the anvil sized fist of the dwarf. Thornberry collapses under the brutal blow, crumpling to the ground.

With a nod of satisfaction, Deron nods at you.

"Never thought I'd collaborate with an elf," Deron spits.

Sheathing their long knives, Lord Raywhen and his son pull back their hoods.

"Evolu," Raywhen says coolly in clarification, yanking the hood from his prisoner. It's Julian—who looks utterly terrified.

"So where's the other accused?" asks the Marshall.

You give a quick whistle. Valda and Dorbane yank Corey into the light, bound and gagged—and with a broken nose.

Dorbane shrugs, but says nothing. Valda shoves him to the ground next to Julian.

"All here and accounted for, sir," you grin.

"Excellent work, young man," Golace nods, then looks at Valda and Dorbane with raised eyebrows. "Excellent work indeed."

- Go to page 190.

15. Save The Soldiers

"Noooo!" you roar, dashing at Gunther. Closing the distance in moments, he turns and raises his sword just in time to block your clumsy blow. You may not be a seasoned soldier, but your aggressive strikes force him back.

There's a loud grunt, and you turn just in time to see Dorbane kicked in the face by the other soldier. The stout Kutollum reels back as his opponent escapes, sprinting into the darkness.

This distraction gives Gunther a momentary advantage...and he disarms you!

Blade at your throat, you stumble backwards onto the ground.

"You have no idea what you're doing!" he hisses, sweating profusely from the pain. "The foreigners are a *curse* upon this land!"

The color has drained from his face. Blood drizzles from the end of his left hand. He stumbles. You scramble in the dry leaves, trying to keep the tip of the sword from penetrating your flesh.

"So you frame innocent people?" you ask, trying to shift his attention.

Gunther pauses, his attention focused on your question. His eyes narrow, "How did you find out about that?"

You never get the chance to answer.

A deep green light appears in the soldiers eyes. A pin of light at first, poking through, followed by a glow emanating from his mouth. He falls forward, onto his knees.

Valda is standing behind him, hand gripping the hilt of her dagger.

Her lips silently repeat the ancient spell of her people, ripping the life force from an enemy and drawing it into her own body. In the flickering light, you can see her cut shoulder also glow green...as the wound slowly *closes*.

Gunther falls forward, face down into the leaves.

Bending over the corpse, Valda pulls her knife free. "Much better," she says, running a finger over the small scar on her shoulder.

You can't help but shudder.

"Remind me not to make you mad," you grunt, getting awkwardly to your feet.

Dorbane stumbles over—pinching his nose. Blood covers the front of his tunic. He looks at both of you and growls, "It was a lucky shot."

Valda stares past you, in the direction where the last soldier fled. When her vision shifts back to you, she looks worried. "We have no idea if these guys have friends out there in the dark."

Before you can respond, you hear a moan from the prone soldier near the campfire.

- To interrogate the captive soldier, go to page 53.
- To go after the fleeing soldier into the night, go to page 80.

16

17.   The Switch

The evening is long and The Three Swords is bursting with patrons until the wee hours of the morning. At the center of the song and celebration is Captain Toma Thornberry and Captain Deron Erdmuth of the Kutollum. The two sit together, buying rounds for their men as Toma makes toast after toast, in honor of the great dwarf warrior. No one ever notices you sitting in the corner of the great hall, sipping warm cider, your hood pulled over your brow.

As the night wanes, the patrons thin out. Soldiers report back to their barracks and few are left conscious in the tavern. It is then that Toma decides to walk his new friend back to the Kutollum barracks, before retiring to his own camp.

"That's not necessary," grins Deron, slapping the human on the back. "The drrinks were enouff...and impressive, I might add!" he slurs.

"N-nonsense," replies Toma, holding the door open. "I know a ssshortcut, used by we portly humans," he leans close to the dwarf and whispers, "who need a b-bit of aid beating our sssoldiers back to camp!"

"M-much obliged, good captain," burps Deron, and they turn down the alley.

Your footsteps are light and sure.

You see no one is about, except the small embers of a pipe in the blackened awning of the stables.

- If you follow Toma, go to page 12.
- If you investigate the light from the pipe, go to page 58.

18. Let Kid Go

"What's your name?" you ask.

He hesitates.

You smile to ease his fear. That, and you elbow Dorbane to stops snarling at the poor kid.

Finally he peeps up. "Filip," he says timidly, "Filip Wellman, from Whitewater."

"Well, Filip Wellman from Whitewater," you sigh, "I think...you're telling the truth."

"You do?" he instantly looks relieved and grateful—especially when Dorbane begrudgingly lowers his axe.

"I do."

You look between your companions, "And I also think you were close to joining those hostages. My gut tells me this Gunther and Keelan weren't going to let this secret walk away with you—even if you did what they asked."

The look of shock on Filip's face is near comical. He shudders, wide-eyed and gapes up at each of you in disbelief. *Not the brightest candle*, you think, *but innocent enough.*

You wink at Valda, who cuts his binds and helps Filip up.

"Throw that tabard into the fire, Filip...and *run*," she tells him. "You can't be a part of this anymore. I don't know how far your farm is from here, but don't stop until you get home."

He looks at each of you, then over at the hostages. "What about them? About Keelan? They'll come after me, and..."

"No, they won't," grumbles Dorbane, "We intend to take care of the rats. Now get on home."

Without pausing, Filip smiles and sprints into the night. "Yes sir!" he calls back, "T-thank you!"

The crunch of the leaves fades into the night.

Valda stares at the bodies. "Now what?" Kneeling by the unconscious young woman, the Gypsy examines her face. She opens the girls mouth. Leaning close, Valda sniffs and instantly recoils. "Ack," blinking her eyes, "Ascroff Root. That smells worse than Grimberries!"

"Explain for those of use who don't know herbs, you tree hugger," Dorbane taunts.

"It's used to control pain. I little can cure a headache, even help with setting a bone, but too much can knock you out. Made into tea or put in boiling water to inhale the vapors—it's potent stuff. I don't know when or how it was administered or even how much. It's impossible to tell. They could be out for hours...even days."

You scratch your head, "We don't have a wagon and we can't carry them all."

"Leave them?" asks Dorbane.

"That wouldn't be wise," you answer, "Keelan might come back, or worse, predators of the four-legged kind."

- Go to page 51.

20. A Mad Gypsy

"You left me!" Valda screams at you, "Lying in a pool of spit!!"

"Hey," laughs Dorbane as you both enter your room, "at least it was *your* spit."

He easily dodges the empty water pitcher as it smashes against the door.

After calming the irate Gypsy, you go over all that you learned...as well as your plan.

She shakes her head in disbelief, "Wow. That is one serious dungheap. And you think this will work?"

You shrug, "What have we got to lose?"

"Quite a lot, actually," she scoffs. "We don't know any of these folks—captains or not, and that Raywhen seems a bit too cool blooded. Elves are supposed to be kind and loving, aren't they?" She gives Dorbane a smirk, "Fellow tree-huggers. Yet your description makes him sound more like Toma. What makes you think any of these players won't turn on us?!"

Dorbane stretches out on the cot in the corner. "It's all we have to go by."

Valda pulls her hair back into a tight ponytail, "So where's Dagan?"

You examine the sword you kept from your original run in with Julian. "Prepping his father for tonight. We're going to need everyone's help to pull this off and still keep the peace."

"So what do you want me to do?" she asks, though she still doesn't look happy.

- "We need you to help Aggie create a distraction to keep Toma in the Tavern until our backup arrives." Go to page 181.
- "I need you to work a little magic." Go to page 17.

22. Next Morning

The morning sun cuts through the leaves and shines warmly on the skin of your face. You open your eyes and yawn. You stretch and yawn again. It was surprisingly a good night—you feel refreshed.

Valda is already up, as are the hostages. She's talking to the young lady. She introduces herself as Aggie. The two older men sit quietly, however, whispering to one another. They smile back when looked at. The young dwarf is sitting alone on a rock at the edge of camp.

Dorbane discovers a few supplies in a discarded sac and distributes the rations to everyone. He takes his share and sits on a stump, watching the sun rise through the trees. You can hear the loud chomping noises as he chews on a hunk of old bread.

The hostages look well enough to travel—so with a little food in your bellies, you pull the tabard from Gunther's cold body and burn it.

No reason to leave this looking like a murder scene.

You leave the body at the base of a tree and cover it with dead branches and loose rocks.

Dorbane nudges you.

"We need to blend in quickly, so no one links us to this camp." He glances at his fellow Kutollum, standing away from the other hostages. "Then we find out what we can. I'll walk with young Dagan, there—see if I can't get some information out of a fellow dwarf, eh?"

"Good idea," you reply.

The Gypsy guides the party back through the trees, helping the young lady—who still seems to be suffering from the effects of the drugs.

- On the walk, you decide to talk to one of the human men... Go to page 49.
- You accompany Valda and decide to strike up a conversation with the young girl, go to page 128.

24. Lord Raywhen

A human visiting an Evolu encampment is one thing, but two Kutollum? It takes more than an hour, with the insistence of Dagan—who boldly declares his royal lineage to the Evolu guards, before you are able to meet with Lord Raywhen.

His quarters are elegant and he is a kind host. You are seated comfortably in plush chairs with delicate cushions, which seems to make your companions uncomfortable. Raywhen listens to your story in full. There is little expression in his demeanor, but he politely waits until you are finished.

"And this is all?" he says calmly.

"All?" you repeat, confused. "Didn't you understand, my lord, what I just said?"

"In full."

"Toma's going to frame my father!" snaps Dagan, shifting uncomfortably in his seat, but controlled.

"Regrettable," Raywhen's tone is cool, "but certainly none of my doing...or concern."

You're shocked at the unemotional response. *I thought Evolu were civilized, loving people?* "You did hear me, that Toma and his accomplices were targeting your own son?"

Raywhen pours himself a glass of wine from a delicate-looking crystal decanter, then lifts the fluted glass to his lips. "Which will be removed from harm, thanks to you."

His lack of emotion is starting to tick you off. "Lord Raywhen, what's to stop Toma from trying again?" Your question causes the elf-lord to pause, momentarily, with his wine glass. He looks deeply into your eyes. "Without working together, there's no evidence to charge Captain Toma with anything. He'll be a free man. A man who hates your kind and could care less that High King Gaston considers your people his kin."

Raywhen sets the glass down on his leaf-pattern desk. "Go on."

You smile...and Dorbane grins wide.

He knows that look.

"I believe, my lord Raywhen," chuckles your best friend, "that my human counterpart has a clever idea."

- If you share your idea and then return to The Three Swords, go to page 20.

- If you share your idea and return with Dagan to his fathers tent, go to page 161.

27. Council With Dorbane

You jab your buddy in the arm and fall behind the group.

"Sounds like this is more than just a couple renegade soldiers," hisses Dorbane, just above a whisper.

You know your stout friend is right, even though you hate to admit it. This whole situation is starting to smell like a nasty plot. The problem is, what can you really do?

"At least we kept five good people from losing their lives," you say.

"Aye."

Aggie seems to be walking fine on her own, so you call Valda over.

"Problem?" she asks.

"Only that I think we're out of our league here," you reply. "Once we hit the Kings Highway, I think it wise we move on."

Valda shrugs.

- "What's wrong, Valda?" Go to page 48.
- "Agreed," says Dorbane, "This is too much heat for three newcomers." Go to page 96.

29. The Boss

Slowly rolling the hay cart back, you're able to kneel down, out of sight, right at the edge of the tent. You can hear someone pacing vigorously on the other side of the cloth from the scuffle of his feet across the rugs.

Suddenly, there is a clatter of shields.

"Are you alright, Captain Toma?" calls one of the soldiers.

"Yes, yes!" snaps the Captain. And then, "You imbeciles!" he hisses in a forced whisper. "Do you have any idea how hard it is to blackmail these damnable foreigners? They're not as stupid as they look!"

"I'm sorry sir." It's Corey's voice. "There was nothing Julian could do—we were ambushed! Gunther was killed and I had to run, or I would have joined him." Corey pauses, then adds, "They had powerful dwarves with them, sir! You know how fierce they are first hand, sir." Another pause, "Five of them..."

So that's your real name...Cory, not Keelan.

Dorbane looks at you cross eyed and bites his knuckles to keep from bursting out in laughter.

"Did you even go back for Gunther's body?" snaps Toma.

There's a span of silence and then Toma growls. "I create the perfect plan to rid our country of this dwarf and elf...filth, and I end up working with idiots!"

"There's nothing to worry about, sir," says Julian cooly. "The girl only saw my face and I can make myself scarce. Lord Raywhen's kid is with those tutors of his until dark, as usual. We've drugged their wine. When they fall asleep, we'll snag the boy and meet you in the alley behind The Three Swords. Get Erdmuth into the alley and we'll do the rest. We can blame Gunther's death on the dwarves as well—as soon as we have the initial leverage. The rest will be easy enough to believe once we create a little prejudice in our favor."

"You...are also smarter than you look, Lieutenant Julian," says Toma.

The tent breaks out into laughter.

"Oh, the look on their faces when Deron Erdmuth is arrested for murdering the son of an Evolu Lord," continues Thornberry, "This tent city will erupt with bloodshed. High King Gaston will be forced to end his treaty for the good of his own people! Andilain will once more be for the human race."

- If you decide to run to Captain Deron Erdmuth, go to page 161.
- If you decide to visit Lord Raywhen, go to page 24.

31. King's Highway

When you reach Cross Point, the sun is high in the sky. A cool breeze carries the scent of merchants on the move. Animals, spices and herbs, leather armor and weapons—the kings highway is already bustling with traffic. Travelers on foot, in cart and wagon, transporting their wares to the capital to sell and trade.

No one pays particular attention to you or any in your party.

Valda nods at the guard house on the far side of the road. It still looks abandoned. "No soldiers."

"Which means," you add, "if Gunther and Keelan were soldiers, this may be their assigned post..."

The two farmers, Blain and Jamel, shake each of your hands gratefully.

"Thank you," says Blain, "We're not likely to find our wagon and it's a long journey home. We have our lives. For that, we will always be grateful."

"Thank you," adds Jamel, with a grin so wide it seems to encompass his small face, "...for everything."

"Take this," you say, tossing the small coin pouch you found on Gunter's body. Blain catches it and frowns, but you nod. "Don't feel bad, he won't be needing it. Call it penance."

With another round of thanks and gratitude, they leave you.

Carts roll past sluggishly, making their way towards Castle Andilain.

"Last chance to ditch this and keep our skins," whispers Dorbane.

- "I don't feel right leaving Dagan and the girl alone and unprotected." Go to page 47.

- "We've done enough. Find a ride for the girl and we'll head to Westgaiden." Go to page 96.

33. Follow Them

"Right," grins Dagan, drool flowing down his chin. He staggers to the bar. Slapping his palm down on the counter, he shouts "Goat Root!"

"Oh, you little devil," chuckles Dorbane, slapping the young Kutollum on the back.

Egerton shakes his head, seemingly disgusted. He lifts a small box onto the counter. Opening it reveals what looks a lot like small, curly, shredded...weeds? You have no clue what it is—but Dagan and Dorbane each take a pinch and put in in their mouths.

Dorbane then takes a pinch and forces his fat fingers between your teeth. Your mouth instantly burns.

"CHEW!" he snaps, and yanks you towards the front door. You follow, though your eyes are already watering.

Your mouth fills with saliva, almost uncontrollably. There's a numbing sensation along your tongue and cheeks.

"Leave the girl in the booth," you yell back at Egerton, "...we'll be right back!"

The three of you get outside just in time to see the two men from the booth. They turn the corner at the far end of the tavern. You start running as fast as you can in pursuit.

Ok, it's closer to aggressive stumbling.

"What is this garbage!??" you complain, "It's disgusting...and it burns!"

"Don't spit it out," warns Dorbane, "just swallow your spit as it forms. It's Goat Root—a rare herb Kutollum use to detoxify animals who get into the Black Lilies we use to make Rum. Our soldiers use it so they can sober up in an emergency. It burns the alcohol from your stomach and blood."

"ARGH!" you wince, grabbing your gut.

"If it doesn't eat a hole in yer stomach first!" says Dagan, who sounds a little too enthusiastic.

Though it's a challenge, the three of you manage to follow Corey and Julian through the maze of structures and up to the outer wall of Castle Andilain. Orderly rows of blue and red tents line the field immediately outside the great walls.

"There!" whispers Dagan, pointing. The Captain's tent. Identified by its size and the two flags posted at it's opening. That and the armed guards.

"I was right," you snarl, "look who our mystery man, Julian is!"

Ducking into the tent flap is Corey and the young farm boy you let go.

"Lying little goat-nut," Dorbane spits.

"Come on," you urge, and work your way around to the horse stables. Several beasts are in a roped off area, which is next to the Captain's tent. There's a hay cart between the tent and the water trough.

- Use the hay cart to hide behind, while you listen at the tent wall. Go to page 29.
- "Let's give those boys a surprise..." Go to page 156.

35. Castle Andilain

Dorbane reaches over and grabs your arm.

"Let him be," he whispers. "He needs to deal with his feelings in his own way."

Right, what was I thinking—that's none of my business. You nod silently and nestle back against the side of the wagon.

Your friend glares back along the road you've traveled. "I'd want revenge on those dung-eating soldiers for what they did to me. If it were me."

Valda kicks your leg from the other side of the wagon and points. "We're here!"

Sure enough, you rise over the last ridge...and into the valley. You can see the massive city of Roland to the south, and up ahead, the famed tent city, surrounding Castle Andilain.

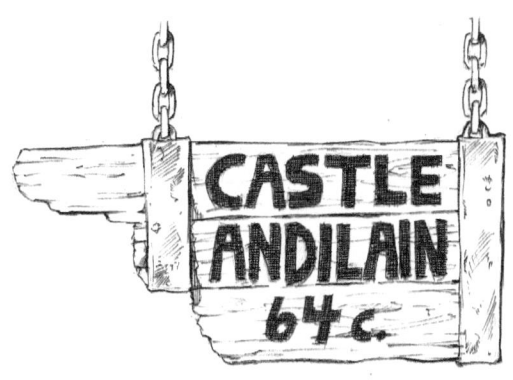

You gawk at the sea of cloth tents covering the open fields once used for agriculture. It's now home to thousands of refugees and two foreign armies.

"So, fearless leader," teases Dorbane, "where to now?"

- "Let's see Dagan safely to his people, then we can escort Aggie to the Tavern." Go to page 44.
- "Let's drop off Aggie at the Tavern and buy Dagan a drink—he looks like he can use it." Go to page 41.

37. Should We Follow?

You wait until the two men leave before you stumble from the booth.

"Wait," huffs Dorbane, staggering across the floor, "we're not sober enough for this."

Dagan falls from the booth onto his face, but immediately struggles to his feet.

"We can't let them get away!" he bellows.

"Dagan's right," you say, burping loudly, "we may not get a second chance at this."

"Well," blurts out Dorbane, "we going or stayin??"

- "Let's do it." Go to page 33.
- Common sense overcomes your bravado. "We'll have to take our chances...we're in no condition to do this." Go to page 166.

38.   Humans?

"Humans?" Deron, exclaimed in shock, "Not cursed Evolu?" Hand on his sword, he glares to you with an intensity that could melt a mountain. "Are you absolutely sure."

Oh, he's definitely looking for a fight. "Positive, sir," you reply respectfully.

Combing his fingers through his long black beard, Deron grunts, "Just my luck."

You all follow with a quiet sigh of relief.

"Which makes Toma's offer something I should consider," adds the Captain.

"Father?" asks Dagan, confused.

Walking to the opposite side of his desk, Deron plops down in a chair. You can't help but admire the workmanship. It's shaped like a sleeping dragon, resting...the arms of the chair made from the folding wings.

"I was a bit...rash," he admits. There is a short pause and then he waves away the looks of his son. "Do not concern yourself, boy. My heart is glad that you are safe and alive. Toma is no friend, to be sure, but I have to mend some fences after the accusations I made. He's...invited me to drink with him tonight." He looks up at you with a smirk and a raised eyebrow. "I suppose I should accept after all."

"If I may, father," asks Dagan, "escort these good people back to The Three Swords? I am sure they are tired after their long journey."

"Of course...of course!" Deron booms, then he stands. His smile is uncommonly warm. He looks to each of you, leaning heavily upon the desk. "You are welcome in my camp,...and you have my personal gratitude for the life of my son."

You turn to leave, when he adds, "If you ever require a favor..."

- If you go to The Three Swords, go to page 41.
- "I think we should find this Captain Toma and inform him about Gunther and Keelan." Go to page 186.

40. Mystery Man

Without thinking, your foot shoots under the table and pins Dorbane's leg.

He starts to growl at you, but you hold a finger to your lips. You nod to the booth behind you.

"What's..." slurs Dagan, but Dorbane slaps a hand over the young Kutollum's mouth.

"Watch what yer doing, Corey!" snaps the voice.

"Sorry," Corey replies quickly, "I'll get the wench..."

"No!" hisses the voice, "Didn't you see the girl? It's the same one you snatched, you idiot! Don't you have eyes?!"

There's a long pause and Valda snorts, rotating her face in her spittle. Yeah...it's not a pretty sight.

"If that girl is back, then those annoying interlopers might be around here too!" You hear a tapping noise, "That would be very bad for us...and Thornberry."

"It's ok, Julian, the Raywhen's kid will be easy pickings. Those Evolu are too trusting. We'll get him tied up and sedated, ready for tonight."

"Then get out! There's too much heat around here until this plan goes down—let's get back to camp."

- If you attempt to follow the two men, go to page 37.
- "That's it," you whisper to Dorbane and Dagan, "let's get these scum!" go to page 159.

41. The Three Swords

The Three Swords is one of the few solid structures you notice throughout the tent city. Erected by the rich merchants of Roland, over one hundred craftsmen and three dedicated architects were employed to build the lodge in a single season. Crafted to entertain eight hundred soldiers in its great hall and house nearly a hundred in the upper rooms, The Three Swords is praised for it's food and its drinks are legendary. Easily considered, during this time of war, one of the most important structures outside the Castle itself.

When you ask Dagan why a tavern would be so important, he responds boldly.

"Because The Three Swords is a tool to soothe the three armies, trying desperately to coexist in peace."

Aggie introduces you to Egerton, the taverns steward. The fat old man is nearly overcome with grief as the young barmaid explains the peril she experienced. He promptly sends her to her room to wash and rest herself—there will be no work for her today. Egerton expresses his profound gratitude to each of you by offering your party a room upstairs. The first week is free of charge.

"Well that was a nice surprise," chimes Valda.

You're all famished and thirsty, so you sit down in one of the many empty booths. The hall is mostly deserted at this time of the morning. The military are performing their drills in the fields. Out of habit, you pull the light red curtain across the opening anyway.

"I really should be getting back," says Dagan.

"Nonsense, lad," chuckles Dorbane, "At least let us buy you one drink. You look like you could use one."

The young Kutollum considers the invitation. "Only one."

Dorbane winks at you, "Of course."

Seven rounds later, you begin to wonder if you're going to be able to find your bed upstairs. That is, if you can find the upstairs at all.

Valda is snoring, face down on the table. Her drool is pooling under her cheek. You only had three pints yourself, but Dagan and Dorbane are still going at it. Slumped in their seats, they order another round and start singing songs of their ravaged homeland. The base pitch of their voices rumbling the liquid in your mug.

All of a sudden, there's a scuffle in the booth next to you. Then the sound of a shattering mug. You see liquid flowing across the wood floor from under the corner of your booths curtain.

"Blast you, Corey!" snaps a familiar voice, "Watch what you're doing, fool!!"

Dorbane's recognized the voice as well...and he's struggling to get out of the booth.

- Pin Dorbane with your foot and keep quiet... go to page 40.
- It's time for payback... go to page 176.

44.   Kutollum

"Let's not leave anything to chance," you say. "Let's get our Kutollum friend back to his people first." Your friends agree.

Dagan leads your party through town and to the formal grounds of the North Camp, home to the Kutollum army. He leads you past two heavily armed guards...and straight to a bright blue tent. The tent is covered in emblems and words you don't understand. It also *dwarfs* the smaller dwellings, you think to yourself.

You try not to laugh.

Hundreds of long-bearded warriors, both working and vigorously training, stare as you cross the grounds. Many smile and even cheer as your new Kutollum friend walks past.

You look at your friends and chuckle. "I'm getting the impression he was missed."

"Or he owes a lot of people money," laughs Dorbane.

But you notice that a few of the soldiers bow as Dagan approaches the tent.

"Who do you think this kid is?" whispers the Gypsy.

The guards at the front of the tent pull back the dragon-crested flaps, admitting you.

"We're about to find out," you mutter.

Dorbane grabs the Gypsy's arm firmly at the entrance. "Don't say a word," he warns her, "You won't be recognized, so don't bother. Don't argue either. It's not personal—it's military. Females don't serve in the ranks. Got it?"

She grumbles, but nods, "Aye."

An older Kutollum walks briskly across the room and up to Dagan. The aged face is sun worn and weathered, an expression of joy plain as day. The young dwarf stands at attention, but keeps his eyes cast at the ground.

"My son!" Wrapping his arms around Dagan like a bear, the soldier hugs him roughly. "Where have you been!? The men searched every inch of this sorry excuse for a city and you were not to be found!" His wise eyes shift to you and Valda, then to Dorbane. His eyes linger on your dwarf friend.

"Father," Dagan breaks off, "I was...taken hostage."

"What?!" Thick black eyebrows furrow like looming storm clouds. His eyes once more shift to you and the Gypsy. He does not look pleased.

"These good strangers saved my life," adds Dagan quickly, "risking their own to do so."

The cold, calculating stare softens instantly and the Kutollum nods at you. "Captain Deron Erdmuth," he announces.

You bow respectfully. "Sir, I am..."

"And who is it that took my son," breathes Deron, cutting you off. His piercing eyes lock on you. Study you.

The two guards inside the tent shift their weapons at the changed tone of their commander. *They're ready to start a fight over this,* you realize. *And he doesn't trust me.* Not good. Luckily, you know exactly what to say.

- "We found two renegade soldiers of Andilain, who had left their post and kidnapped four of their own race. They had your son captive as well." Go to page 113.

- "They were human, sir, but..." Go to page 38.

47. Wagon Ride

Traveling to Andilain goes by fast enough. You tip a wine bibber a silver coin for a semi-comfortable ride in the back of his wagon.

Dagan, the young Kutollum, is silent for hours. His attention is pulled towards the forest along the road as the wagon bounces up the pot-riddled road. You've seen that look on Dorbane's face more than once: *pride*.

He's embarrassed about these events, you think...*and probably in a world of trouble, once he get's back to the city.*

- "None of this is your fault, you know." Go to page 35.
- You give Dagan his space and you shut your eyes the rest of the ride to Andilain. Go to page 116.

48.   What's Wrong?

"This isn't like you," she says, disappointed. "Ever since we were kids, you did what was right. Mahan's panties— you even pushed me to spend summers with my own people and learn the ways of *The Whisper*."

"Yeah," you say, "and I'm never sure if I should feel bad about that."

Dorbane laughs.

"Haw-haw," she mocks, sticking out her tongue at the Kutollum. "These are innocent people. We don't actually know if there's someone else behind it all. What if they find out—especially once we get Dagan and Aggie back to their homes? Surely they'll be noticed?"

You hadn't thought about that.

The idea of being hunted or killed by thugs in the shadows of an unfamiliar city flash through your mind. "Being found dead in an alley...or ANYwhere for that matter, doesn't sound encouraging."

You look at your Kutollum friend and realize Dorbane is thinking the same thing.

"We're screwed," you say in unison.

- Ah, well...life's too short to give into fear. Go to page 31.
- You decide to save your skins and abandon your plans for Andilain. Go to page 120.

49.   Blain And Jamel

You soon learn the two older humans are brothers. Blain and Jamel...both farmers from Whitewater. They were traveling to Castle Andilain to sell their grain to the army.

"It's been a good year for us," smiles Blain, "so we filled our cellar for the winter. When we saw, for once, that we had more than enough—we thought the surplus might help our soldiers, while putting some much needed coin in our pockets."

Jamel scratches his head, openly disappointed, "Only, we never thought we'd be waylaid!"

You grumble, "You couldn't have known."

"That's what's so disturbing," adds Blain. He catches himself on a small tree as you push through the forest, "You get so fixated on the enemy out there," he waves his hand wildly, "that you never consider your own race might be bad."

It's a disturbing though, you agree. "So how did you both get kidnapped?" you ask, intrigued. "That seems a bit odd, if you don't mind my saying so."

Jamel shrugs. "We were stopped to be inspected," he says, "With the war going on, we didn't argue."

Dorbane, walking just ahead of you and listening, shakes his head. "But there are two of you," he says out loud, "How did the soldiers get you both without a fight?"

The brothers look at one another, embarrassed. Finally, Blain mutters, "They gave us hot tea, to take the chill out of our bones."

Both you and Dorbane can't help but laugh out loud.

49

"Drugged and out cold in moments," spat Jamel, "all 'cause we thought those boys were being polite."

- You accompany Valda and decide to strike up a conversation with the young girl, go to page 128.
- If you decide to talk to Dagan, go to page 123.
- You have a private word with Dorbane, go to page 27.

51.   Make Camp

"Our best option is to camp here," you say, resigned.

"What's eating at you?" asks Dorbane, "You seem...worried."

You have a nagging feeling inside, alright. "If soldiers of Andilain are committing crimes against their own people..." you dread the very thought, "Then where will that leave us, once we get to Andilain? I came to fight against evil, not join it."

"Its something we need to get to the bottom of," says Valda reassuringly. "I'd wager these are rogues, so don't count out our countrymen just yet."

It makes sense and you nod—but the uneasy feeling doesn't go away.

Valda pats your shoulder. "I'll take first watch, since I'm the most *refreshed*. She winks at Dorbane.

"You really creep me out when you suck people dry like that," he shudders.

She grins at the Kutollum and makes smacking sounds with her mouth, "Tastes like chicken."

"Seriously," Dorbane winces, "Eww."

You laugh.

Riffling over Gunther's corpse, you collect his weapons and coin. You find a sizable bag of silver. *Payment, perhaps? This a lot of coin to be carrying around.* Leaving his body at the base of a tree, you gently move the hostages closer to the fire, where they can be watched, kept warm and safe.

Valda does take the first watch. Like a forest cat, she silently climbs one of the nearby trees, disappearing among the limbs. If anyone tries to sneak up on the camp, they'll be in for a surprise.

Dorbane curls up with his axe by the fire and immediately drops off into slumber.

- With a little effort, you set aside your concerns and close your eyes…go to page 22.
- Something about this whole situation bothers you deeply. You go for a walk to think it through in private. Go to page 64.

53.   Interrogate Soldier

Cutting the ropes from the hostages, you use the cord to bind the waking soldiers hands and feet. Propping him up against a tree stump and facing the fire, you get a good look at him.

He's just a kid!

Worn, thin, dirty faced...and now with a black and purple welt across the side of his head.

What seems strange to you...is his clothes. You look at him curiously.

"Is it me, or does this guy look out of place?"

Valda scoffs, "He's a killer, preying on his own people,...what do you expect?"

"No," you clarify, "look at his clothes. They don't fit him by a long shot." You look over at Gunther's body. "He doesn't have armor underneath. In fact...he doesn't even have a sheath for his sword."

The soldier's eyes flutter open and he immediately recoils, staring directly at you.

"AHH!" he screams, "Please don't hit me! I didn't do it, I swear I didn't do anything wrong!"

"Do what?" you ask cooly.

"Whatever it is you tied me up for!" the young man cries out. He looks at the bodies still lying against the hillside. "Are they...?"

"They're alive," grumbles Dorbane, "No thanks to you."

The soldier sighs heavily, letting his head roll forward. His body shakes and at first you think he's laughing—but he starts to sob. "I'm so glad..." he weeps uncontrollably, "So glad."

The three of you are seriously confused and glance between one another.

"I didn't want to have anything to do with this," he whines, "They said they'd kill my mother if I didn't help them." He pouts like a child when he looks at Valda. "Life has been so hard on the farm and with my father gone..."

He looks up at you pleadingly, "I swear, I didn't know what was going on! You have to believe me—all they told me I had to do, was dress in this soldier costume and watch the traitors."

The pain and anguish in his face looks real enough...and he keeps looking over at the unconscious bodies. Maybe he's telling the truth.

His voice drops to a near whisper, filled with desperation. "When I heard Gunther and Keelan talking about killing those people, I ran! Keelan caught me and hit me over the head."

You nod at Valda. She pushes the soldiers head forward and inspects it. "Nice goose egg on the back of his head. You hit him from the front."

He looks away, into the darkness, "He dragged me back and...when I woke up, he said if I ran again, he'd slit my throat."

- I think the kid is innocent and telling the truth, go to page 18.
- You decide to rough the kid up, to make sure he's not lying, go to page 134.

56. Rush The Soldiers

"I'll create a distraction," you say, scrambling to your feet.

You have but moments to act.

Dorbane grips his axe and Valda slips her jeweled knife from her belt. Unfortunately, all you have is the tree limb you've been using as a walking stick. *Not much against swords*, you think to yourself, *but it'll have to do.*

"Spread out," you whisper, then push off the fallen log and dash around the tree line. Your heart is pumping, your mind reeling for ideas.

...the soldier is mere feet away from his victims.

It is then that you notice a sword, stuck in the ground next the soldier by the fire. It's also without a sheath. The soldiers back is still turned to you. The other two haven't noticed you moving about. Suddenly, you see Valda creeping into the camp from the opposite side, her knife in hand.

It's now or never, you think...and dash towards the sword.

"HEY—YOU!!" shouts the soldier closest to Valda. Drawing his own sword, he runs towards you, completely missing the Gypsy. This grabs the attention of the soldier now leaning over the prisoners...but it also alerts the man sitting by the fire.

You reach him just before the soldier can grab his sword and pull it free.

With all your might, you swing your walking stick. It connected with him squarely across the jaw. There's a sickening crack and the man spins...and collapses to the ground.

The body doesn't move.

56

"Kill them now, Gunther!" you hear someone yell. Instinctively, you drop the stick and pull the sword free with both hands.

A second shout cuts through the night air. One of pain. The soldier called Gunther, the one near the prisoners, has dropped his knife. Valda's small blade protrudes from his left shoulder, buried to the hilt. Reaching, grasping desperately to get to the source of pain, the soldier can't reach the weapon. He stumbles and moans, but doesn't fall.

"A little help here!" cries Valda, dodging sword swings from the third soldier. You can see a fresh cut across her arm, blood seeping from her elbow.

Before you can react, you hear the war cry of a Kutollum. A deep roar of a furious beast that would cause a bear to take flight.

Dorbane bursts into the firelight, swinging his axe.

"Strike at a girl!?" he screams in rage, "A child!??" The soldier barely deflects the powerful blows in time. "You coward! You,...you...*donkey dung!!*"

You start to grin, but your attention is immediately drawn to a flash of movement. From the corner of your eye, you catch a glimpse of Gunther.

He has drawn his sword with his uninjured arm...and is about to execute the prisoners.

- Go to page 15.

58. Investigate The Light

Quickly stepping into the shadows, you nod to Marshall Golace.

"This is a serious accusation," he whispers, "I hope your hunch proves correct."

"I'm grateful you came at all, Marshall," you reply.

"I wouldn't have, if it wasn't for Lord Raywhen vouching for you. He's not easily swayed...or impressed, but he seemed to be taken with your determination."

You grin to yourself. "I'll take what I can get."

- Go to page 12.

59. Follow Trail

"Let's check this out," you say quietly. It could be the guard in trouble. Perhaps a merchant. The fact is, something is going on and you want to know what that is.

Stealthily moving across the road and up to the ridge, you stop. You quickly check the tree line for signs of life. Nothing. The three of you then crawl up to the peak and look down into the forest.

The trees are dense, but Valda taps you on the shoulder. She points northwest. There's a path through the brush. Two distinct lines through pine needles and mud...made by a body being dragged across the ground.

"Not exactly the brightest candle, now is he?" whispers Dorbane sarcastically. You have to smile.

"Spread out," you whisper, "I'll walk the path."

Both Dorbane and Valda nod and slip over the ridge, vanishing into the shadows of the trees.

Luckily there's enough moonlight to discern your general whereabouts. You slowly, cautiously, make your way through the forest--paying close attention to the sounds around you. For several minutes you keep silent. That is, until you hear a voice.

You can't see either of your friends, so you crouch low, making your way through the underbrush as quickly as possible.

There is a flicker of light in the distance.

A fire.

- If you sneak up on the campsite, go to page 87.
- If you decide to look for Dorbane and Valda, go to page 10.

61. Stay Together

"Let's stick together," you caution, "there's no telling what he can do...and we don't know how well he might know this forest."

All three of you sprint into the night—in the direction the last soldier fled. It's not long before you're forced to stop, however. The forest curves and slopes downward towards a lake. The only other safe path leads along the mountainside.

Both paths look worn with frequent use.

"Blast!" you curse, "He could have taken either path."

Valda stares down the slope at the water of the broad lake. "If he has a boat, the lake will be the surest escape."

"Agreed," replies Dorbane, "but the path into the mountains would make it easier to hide. Rocks mean no trails. If he went this way, we'll need to catch him soon."

- If you follow the mountains, go to page 109.
- If you go to the lake, go to page 153.

62. Getting Food And Drink

The Three Swords is one of the few solid structures in the tent city. Erected by the rich merchants of Roland, over a hundred woodsman and three architects were employed to erect the lodge in a single season. Built to house eight hundred soldiers in its great hall, The Three Swords caters to the three armies which surround it. The armies, trying desperately to coexist in peace.

It's mid morning and there are few patrons in the great hall. You find a secluded booth in the back and stretch out.

Valda orders a round of drinks and a large platter of eggs and steak from the fat Innkeeper. You're all sore from the long walk through the night and it feels good to have food in your stomachs.

You have a few more rounds and decide to get a room for the night.

"Best to show up looking like we're actually worth our weight in food," grumbles Dorbane, yawning.

"Right," adds Valda, "enlisting will come soon enough. I'm dead tired."

But before you get up, you hear some swearing in the booth next to you.

"It ain't right I tell you!" says a voice.

"Keep yer tone down, ya blasted coot!" hisses another, "Ya wanna get caught? That's a charge of murder! ...you wanna hang, do ya?"

There's a long pause, and then softer, "Course not, Sargent."

"Then keep yer damned trap *shut!*" the sargent snaps, "Drink up,...we's got work to do, boy. Keelan and Gunther've prolly gutted those folks b'now. Not long b'fore they frame that nasty Kutollum brat."

You glare at Dorbane. He starts to rise, but you shake your head. "Hear them out," you whisper.

"You think this is really gonna work, Sarge?" the voice continues, "What if the dwarves just start a war against us? Ever think of that?"

The sargent laughs, then you hear the sound of a mug being slammed on a table. "Toma's got a plan fer that too! Screw those elves right proper, he will! Get ALL these foreigners outta our lands. Now let's go."

- If you decide to ignore the conversation and enlist in the morning, go to page 106.
- If you decide to follow the sergeant and his young friend, go to page 76.

64. Something About This Whole Situation

There's something that keeps bothering you, itching at the back of your mind. You decide to go for a walk, while everyone sleeps, to try and work this out.

The moon is out and the crickets are chirping in the night air.

You stroll deeper into the trees.

Why would anyone want to drug civilians and kidnap them? Why try to kill them? But what really bothers you is: why involve a Kutollum in all this? If it ever got out that a Dwarf had killed humans on purpose....

That's IT!

It's only then, that you notice the crickets have...gone silent.

You never hear the footsteps. The rock hits you in the back of the head.

Your body falls heavily to the ground.

Hands roll you onto your back. In the scattered moon light, you can barely make out the blurry face of Filip.

He smiles.

"Thanks for letting me go," he whispers. "My boss will be so happy to know that his plan is still in play."

He straddles your chest, covers your mouth with one hand...and with the other, slides a long dagger between your ribs.

THE END

65. Report To Sergeant Stewart

You are led to a dirty, old, leaning tent that's seen better days. When you pull back the flap and step inside, both you and Valda raise your eyebrows.

Sergeant Stewart isn't what you expected.

He looks old. *Too* old—at least to be serving in the military. He looks more likely to fall off the barrel he's straddling, than to stand at attention. His whole head, including his bald scalp, is a collection of wrinkles, without beginning or end. The narrow distance from his chin to the tip of his nose tells you he's toothless. He has a short stem pipe in his mouth, a steady stream of smoke rolling up into the air as he puffs away on it.

"Right," he says in a gravel tone, "two new recruits, eh? Who sentcha?"

"Rodrick McDonnell, sir," you answer.

"Did he now..." Sergeant Stewart looks you both up and down, then slaps down two tabards. He issues you and Valda a pair of nicked, worn swords. The leather is dry and torn...and even the mouthpiece on the scabbards show signs of rust.

Valda raises her eyebrows, "Uh,..okaaay."

You give her a warning glance—to say nothing.

"You'll be in row four, tent twelve." He looks at both of you. "You don't have a problem sharing the same quarters?" He shakes his head, "Not that I agree with females in the military, but if they want to serve, we ain't got no time to roll out carpets or douse cots with flower buds."

Valda grits her teeth, holding back her usual, charming snarl. "I grew up in the woods. Slept in trees, caves and other places you *men*-folk wouldn't dare go."

Stewart laughs, "Ooooo, ain't she the feisty one? HAH! We can use that, we can!"

Great, you cringe, *my confidence in the military is growing by the moment*.

"Now," Stewart snaps, "get suited up and report to the stables in an hour, your group leaves for your first assignment today."

Valda looks at you, not only confused, but annoyed. You have to admit, you're feeling the same way.

"Sir," you ask, "What assignment?"

Stewart just gives you an ominous grin.

- If you show up as ordered, go to page 102.
- This just doesn't feel right—we should be trained...or something before going out. Go to page 69.

67. Fight Gunther

You hold your hands up in surrender.

Gunther smiles, pulling a long knife from his hip.

"D-don't hurt me," you plea, hands shaking.

Come closer, you moron. That's it...cloooooser.

As the soldier steps in range, you roll to the side, pushing off the ground with your hands. This gives you the momentum to kick him across the calves, knocking Gunther's legs out from under him.

The knife goes flying through the air while the soldier lands squarely on his back. You hear the wind knocked from him with a loud OOOF!

Hoping to your feet, you notice Dorbane bolting into the light, axe swinging at the other guard. He lets out his Kutollum battle cry, piercing the night air.

This, however, get's the attention of the soldier by the campfire! *Oh no!*

Kicking Gunther across the face in passing, you scoop up a tree branch from the ground and dash towards the fire.

He doesn't notice me...come on legs, faster, blast you!

You push yourself forward. With a mighty swing, you strike the soldier across the jaw—knocking the helmet clean off his head, and rendering him unconscious. The body flips back over the log and onto the ground, face down.

You're breathing hard, but you see Valda sprinting into the light, running towards you. Even in the dim light, you can see her eyes are wide with fear.

"Stop him!" she yells, pointing to the hostages.

You spin around.

Gunther is staggering towards the bodies, a sword drawn.

He's going to kill them!

- Go to page 15.

69.   This Just Doesn't Feel Right

"Sir," you add as you leave.

Stewart looks up at you, pulling the pipe from his mouth and smacks his gums. "What is it, soldier?"

Valda shakes her head.

You continue anyway.

"This seems, well...highly suspect, sir." Glancing out the tent flap, you can plainly see recruits being trained. "We haven't been prepared for combat, or, for anything, except maybe the most menial of duties. We've never served in the military before, but it does seem strange to be sent out on an assignment so fast...doesn't it?"

Your Sargent raises a wild, grey eyebrow, considering your words carefully.

"Maybe you're right," he smiles.

Valda breathes a sigh of relief.

"I'm glad we have alert, conscientious people noticin' the details o' things. I got just the duty for you...and it won't take no training at all."

You and Valda spend the next six months exclusively as stable hands. From dawn until dusk, you shovel horse manure.

Valda...isn't very happy with you.

THE END

70. Run

Rolling to your feet, you sprint as fast as you can, across camp and into the darkness.

You're young, you're fast and you're not wearing armor to slow you down!

...what you *don't* anticipate in your panic, however, is your eyesight.

Dashing immediately from firelight into darkness didn't allow your sight to adjust...and you trip over a shrub, falling forward. You stumble, trying to catch yourself—but your head finds something to steady you first:

A tree.

Knocked senseless, you collapse.

...the sound of footsteps close in.

You hear Dorbane call your name, then his war shout. The screams of Valda aren't far behind. You look about, but your eyes won't focus.

A large shadow blots out the firelight in the distance.

You feel a sharp pain in your head and all goes black.

....you awake to the sound of water. Oars. Rowing.

"Lake Mead is one of our natural beauties," says Gunther. "It's the one place I can come to find peace and quiet."

You try to move, but you can't. You're tied too firmly with ropes. Bound with the unconscious bodies of Valda and Dorbane.

"You won't get away with this," you spit.

Gunther smiles. "You know, everyone told me I was just a millers boy—that I would never amount to anything but grinding flour." He stops rowing. "But that goes to show the narrow thinking minds of today's society. They just don't see using talents outside their station."

Reaching over, he pats a large circular stone by your feet.

"But see here—a mill stone can be used for more than just grinding flour."

Your stomach sinks as you connect the dots.

"Oh yes," he whispers, "I do think he's figured it out."

Looping the thick rope through the mill stone, the soldier smiles.

"I'm glad we had this little chat."

With a grunt, he shoves the stone into the water, the length of rope disappearing behind it. Gunther leans against the opposite side of the boat and gives you a final wink.

"I'd hold my breath if I were you."

You and your friends are yanked into the depths of the ice cold lake and plummet to the bottom, where you are held fast.

You struggle, holding your breath for as long as you can, but it's no use.

THE END

72.   You Follow The Two Soldiers

They're not going to get away with this, you think to yourself.

"I know that look," whispers Valda. She sighs. "I'm ready when you are."

"No signatures, no training, no real weapons or uniforms issued," you spit, "which means this is a setup."

The Gypsy's eye glint in the dim starlight, her fingers tapping on the hilt of her dagger. "I'd like some payback."

"As would I," you growl. You locate a fallen branch. It's perfect as a walking stick...*and may come in handy when applied to some heads*, you grin.

"Right, let's go cause some trouble."

You follow the ridge of the mountain range, keeping to the deep shadows as you go. Before long, you smell the sweet scent of bourbon tobacco in the air.

You tap Valda on the shoulder. She notices the scent as well.

There's a small snap of a tree limb in the distance...and then you hear the soft singing...

...of Kutollum folk-songs.

"What the blazes are you doing out here in the woods?" you snap at Dorbane as you barge into the open moonlight.

The Kutollum jumps from the tree log he'd been leaning against and grabs you both, hugging you like a bear. "MY FRIENDS!"

"Shhhhh!" stammers Valda, slapping a hand over Dorbane's mouth. "We're tracking murderers!" She motions to the cover of a group of trees. Dorbane and you follow.

"Why are you out here, Dorbane?" you ask.

His head sways back and forth, embarrassed, "I didn't have the heart to join up, once I heard they were shipping new recruits back North. With my family gone, Andilain's become my new home—though I do miss the snow." He smiles brightly, and you can see his teeth, even in the shadows. "I didn't have anywhere else to go, so I thought I'd walk for a spell. Maybe head back to the orphanage," he winks at Valda, "Maybe find two new youngsters to raise into fine members of society."

She moans.

"Well, we're tracking two men who like *killing* fine members of society." You poke the dwarf in the chest, "Which is something you'd probably like to do something about, yes?"

His look shifts to the cold reality of business.

Gripping his axe, "There's a camp not far from here." Dorbane grins menacingly, "What's say we drop in for a visit?"

So as not to be caught unaware, the three of you spread out and make your way towards the firelight you see in the distance.

- Go to page 10.

74. Try To Wake A Hostage Up

All of this is moving too fast—there's not enough time. No plan, no way to prepare...lives at stake.

But something pricks your mind.

There's a reason your friends follow you. A reason you gained the respect of an entire village...even though you were a lowly orphan. You are driven to do what's right, because it's right—not because it's easy or convenient. You've defended others from wolves, bears, raiders and even invading clans.

...three soldiers you can do.

Right, you tell yourself, crazy or not, we all go home tonight.

Crawling quietly through the brush, you make your way around the camp and up the ridge, above the embankment. Maybe I can wake them?

With Gunther and the others distracted, it doesn't sound like such a bad plan. Not a good plan,...but not terrible.

There's a roar from the far side of the camp and Dorbane jumps into the light, swinging his axe. The leader rolls from the stone and sparks fly as the axe glances of it. Gunther draws his sword and runs towards the fray.

A scream then splits the night air as Valda dashes from the shadows nearby. She's wielding a tree branch and swings it with all her might at the soldier by the campfire. The soldier reaches for his sword, but is met by the wood—knocking his helmet clean off his head. The body flips backwards, feet over head.

That girl is insane!

You're already on your feet and sliding down the embankment. Her attack catches Gunther's attention...and he turns on the Gypsy.

Valda see's you and flings her crude weapon in your direction, spinning past Gunther's first thrust of his sword. Her hand grabs at the sword standing near the fire, but the trained soldier spins with her, blade slicing deep through her arm.

She screams.

Red flows down her arm and it goes limp. Gunther follows up with a punch to Valda's face, sending her sprawling onto the ground.

He's going to kill her!

You snatch the branch from the ground and race to save your best friend.

- Go to page 15.

76.   You Follow the Sergeant

You get a profile glimpse of the sergeant as he passes. Old, smoking a pipe, hunch—the young man is skinny and blonde, both wearing the red and blue tabards of Andilain. They stop at the bar, where the old man flirts a bit with an older barmaid.

"I have no intention of joining a bunch of cutthroats!" you exclaim.

Dorbane slams his fist down on the table with such force, the mugs jump. "And I'll not allow a fellow dwarf to fall at the hands of traitors!"

Valda yawns, "At least Andilain isn't boring."

You wait for the two men to leave and slip out after them. Not knowing the town, you have to keep right on their heels as they weave in and out of the tents and temporary shelters erected by merchants.

"Do you see them?" you ask Valda.

She shakes her head, then kicks a rock. "We lost them. Blast!"

Dorbane points ahead, "No, I think that's them...right there—come on!"

The three of you sprint and round an armor merchant and into a blacksmith's building. The wide open doors are extended outward—giving the illusion of walls. The building is deep, the loud ring of the hammer on steel echoes in your ears. The blacksmith glances up at you between blows, but doesn't say a word.

You see the doors are open on the other end of the building and motion Valda and Dorbane to follow.

"Well, well, well, what do we have here?" says the sergeant, stepping into the opening. "Looks like a dwarf and two foreign-lovers to me." He looks to his side and large men in solid red tunics step into the opening. "What do you think, gentlemen?"

"Aye," says a black haired brute, standing nearly seven feet in height. He taps a heavy mace in the palm of his hand, "Foreign-lovers they are."

"Shame," says the red headed human with a broken nose, "I hate messing up the faces of pretty girls." He glares at Valda and licks his lips.

The doors suddenly close behind you and you hear the sound of a heavy plank being lowered into place. The blacksmith continues to strike the hot metal on his anvil.

You're trapped.

- Try to yell for help. Go to page 97.
- Stand and fight. Go to page 94.

78. Loop Around And Hide Near The Hostages

You lead the three soldiers into the darkness, casting stones one after another. When they decide to go back, you let out a small growl, imitating a Tailmain. The sound of the nasty nocturnal predator puts them on the defensive and they reposition themselves, placing their backs against one another.

This gives you the opportunity to quietly make your way back to the hostages. As you get closer to the light, you can see the bodies slumped against the far embankment. You grit your teeth.

This is wrong on so many levels.

They look so innocent and fragile.

What are these beasts doing? Traitors! The thought of honor bound soldiers placing the lives of innocent citizens in danger irks you. But this is worse—these people have been kidnapped!

You have to act fast. Get around to the other side of the camp—get to these people and get them out of here. You don't know why you feel such an obligation, you don't even know who they are. But you do feel an obligation.

A soft chirp catches your attention.

Valda! But you can't see her as you scan the tree line. *Dorbane should be nearby too.*

Another mixture of chirps and you know exactly what to do—*hide!*

Moments later, the soldiers come back.

They stomp into camp, the smallest of the three sinking back down onto the log at the fire—plunging his sword into the dirt next to him.

"Gunther!" snaps the largest of the soldiers, "Slit their throats...or I'll slit yours!"

The big man, apparently the leader, walks to the opposite edge of the camp and sits down on a rock. He pulls a sack onto his lap and starts searching.

Gunther starts talking to the soldier hunched near the fire.

Now is the only chance you're going to have!

- Untie the hostages, go to page 91
- Try to wake a hostage up, go to page 74

80. Go After The Escaping Soldier

"This is crazy," you grunt, "we can't let that guy get away. There's no telling what he could do to us—here or in Andilain, if we're not careful."

Dorbane snaps his nose back into place with a twitch and a curse. "We go after him then?"

"Absolutely."

The dwarf points to the stirring soldier on the ground, "What about him?"

"I've got it," Valda says.

With a swift motion, she stomps on the end of a tree branch, flipping the opposite end into the air for her to grab. With a single thump across the back of his head, the soldier stops moving.

"Seriously," you stress to Dorbane, "don't let me tick her off."

- If you split up to cover more ground, go to page 155.
- If you stick together, go to page 61.

81.   Lost Much?

Thank you for submitting your application for a part in our *Find-Your-Way* game.

We received many responses and are sadly unable to accept them all.

We wish you well as an invisible passage and hope that someone else finds a use for you.

If anyone stumbles upon you by accident please redirect them to the last passage they were at.

Have a nice day.

82. Report The Incident To The Authorities

Without delay, you run from the area and into the courtyard of Castle Andilain. You insist on speaking to one of the Royal Guard—the elite soldiers of High King Gaston.

When you mention murder, you finally get an audience with Marshall Golace. He seems to be a fair man and he patiently listens to your adventures and accusations.

...unfortunately, you have no real proof. Two dead bodies are recovered, and there are several witnesses, including the blacksmith, that testify the three of you entering the shop and closing the doors.

You are tried and convicted...for murder.

What's worse, you're found guilty of murdering men under the Marshall's own stewardship...with the involvement of a Kutollum. Before a scandal can arise, you are all executed. High King Gaston makes it a public event, which satisfies the hunger for justice among the people.

Your heads now hang from the castle walls. Displayed over the three military camps as an example.

Violence between races will not be tolerated.

THE END

83. Run Towards The Kings Highway

Awww, crap, you curse. You're not thinking fast enough —they're rushing towards the sounds…they'll be on top of you any moment!

Just going to have to hope Valda and Dorbane get to the hostages quickly.

You sprint away, kicking up leaves and stomping through the brush so even a deaf hunter could find you. The goal is to make your way to the kings highway.

When the torches stop, you loop around, making threatening sounds of a Tailmain, giving the impression that a beast is on the prowl. That's the danger with Tailmain—they're cold-blooded killers. A feared night predator, they have to be taken out before they sneak up in the dark and attack you. You know this will spur them on.

The soldiers are forced to pick up their pace. Woah, woah, WOAH! you panic, ducking low and diving under some dense bushes. Then they sprint towards you, swords drawn, torches in hand.

Before the light can reveal where you're hidden, you throw a well-placed rock crashing through the underbrush, yards away.

The light instantly navigates away from you.

Dropping your face into your hands, you sigh in relief.

Way too close.

You lie still for a while, listening carefully. You hear shouts in the distance. *They're trying to find the beast that doesn't exist.* You know they'll give up when they can't find it—it's too dangerous to leave hostages alone.

When all feels quiet, you venture back to the camp…and sure enough, the soldiers have returned and taken their posts. The hostages are still lying against the embankment. *Blast!*

Where are Valda and Dorbane?!

- Go to page 10.

85. You Are Captured

You put up a good fight, but the odds are not in your favor.

You're captured and taken, bound and gagged...to Captain Toma Thornberry.

He looks down upon you with disdain.

"Shame," he mutters, more to himself than to you, "could have used someone like you, with spirit." He lifts a wine glass, taking a sip, then smiles. "But I can't have my plans interrupted by a outsider...even if you are one of my own race."

Four soldiers take you out by moonlight and beat you until you can barely stand. Just when you think it's over, your heart stops.

...there's an Evolu rapier protruding from your chest.

Your body is left near the Evolu camp. You're discovered by the Royal Guard the next morning, during the watch change. A scandal starts to which the elves have little to say in their own defense.

Civil war erupts. The Kutollum gladly join the humans against the elves...

THE
END

86.   This Doesn't Exist

You must have fallen off the trail into a forbidden area, as no route leads here, and from here there is nowhere to go.

If you are lucky you may be able to climb back to where-ever you came from, and with luck you might make a better choice than you did last time.

However, there is nothing to see here, so please move along. We wish you well on your journey.

87.   Sneak Up On Camp Site

The moisture in the leaves help muffle the sound of your footsteps. You've been hunting in the hills most of your life, trapping small and medium sized game—you know how to sneak. However, not all Kutollum have such skills.

You can hear Dorbane tromping through the brush in the distance. Fortunately, a sharp hiss from Valda silences him.

You drop low as you approach the light of the fire.

There are three men. One soldier is hunched over, sitting on a fallen log by the fire. He's a small man, skinny, his sword unsheathed, stuck into the ground next to him. Two others—bigger, heavily armed, stand next to what looks like...bodies?

There's more than one?

The two soldiers are arguing, but you can't understand what they're saying. You search the rim of the light around the camp, but you don't see any sign of your friends.

Where are you guys?

All three men are wearing the blue and red tabard of Andilain. Your stomach sinks—this is not good. Are these traitors? Thieves?

"Stop squirming, Gunther!" growls the bigger soldier. With two fingers, he shoves his comrade back and points at him warningly. "You slit their throats...or I'll slit yours!"

The soldier, called Gunther, makes a foul gesture at the mans back as he walks away. He then shuffles over to the man by the fire. Again, there is conversation that you can't hear—because of their hushed tones. The thin soldier remains hunched over. He never looks up.

Now's your chance!

- Maybe you can untie the hostages! Go to page 91.
- Create a distraction and draw the soldiers away, go to page 90.

89. Make Animal Sounds To Draw Them Away

Backing away from the perimeter of the camp, you cup your hands and start making the growling sounds of a Tailmain.

For once, your talent for imitating the dog-sized mammal can be used for something other than scaring the girls in the outhouse late at night. Known for their aggressive night hunting, these thick skinned predators have to be dealt with before they attract their packs to assist it.

You pause, letting the worry—the panic—to set in. Then you take a deep breath and let out a gnarled howl...the sound a Tailmain makes when it thinks it's found a food source.

It works!

In moments, all three soldiers have grabbed torches and swords, rushing to the edge of the camp. They venture out, slowly, towards you.

You let out a grunt, scraping through the leaves with your boot. They turn in your direction. You can't help but smile—this is too easy...

Then you realize you've stood still too long.

They're almost on top of you!

- Run towards the kings highway, go to page 83
- Run deeper into the forest, go to page 95.

90. Draw The Soldiers Away

Let's see if we can stir up some paranoia, you grin to yourself.

Getting some distance, you feel through the leaves and gather a few stones and a couple pieces of wood.

Tossing the heaviest stone towards camp, you can see the soldier by the fire jump.

Oh yeah—that startled him!

The soldier calls to his comrades and looks out towards the area of darkness, where the rock landed. You know he can't see anything—especially after staring too long into the fire.

But that's the point...to use the unseen.

The other two soldiers dash to the edge of the camp, their swords drawn.

Another well placed rock nearby makes them all jump...and the game is on.

- Make towards the kings highway, go to page 83.
- Loop around and hide near the hostages, go to page 78.

91.   Untie The Hostages

I can't let them kill innocent people, you convince yourself.

Your friends are nowhere to be seen and you can't wait any longer—Gunther will surely kill those people at any moment.

Taking a deep breath, you sneak around the rim of the camp and climb up the embankment, keeping to the trees. There are four bodies, all with sacs over their heads.

Three men and...a woman??

Those bastards!

They're laying up against the embankment, hands tied behind backs. You look over at the fire. Gunther is still there.

Probably complaining about being stuck with a murder's lot.

You slip through the shrubs on your belly and weave like a snake down through the tree line, towards the hostages. Taking hold of a small sapling, you slowly lower yourself down the embankment, trying not to grunt with the strain. You get within arms reach of the bodies.

Just as you look back to pull a small knife from your boot, you hear a sound.

"Ahem."

You look up to see Gunther, standing in front of you—his evil grin makes the deep scar across his right cheek look like an extra fold of skin.

Oh crap.

Startled, you lose your grip and tumble down the embankment. You stop rolling at Gunther's feet.

"It looks like I have five bodies to deal with now," he growls.

- If you decide to fight Gunther, go to page 67.
- If you decide to run, go to page 70.

93.   You Die

Bad News: Your plan doesn't work. You die.

Good News: Your death is a convenient one.

A large shipment of the finest ale is delivered to the Kutollum soldiers as a peace offering. There is a great celebration in the dwarf camp. During the wee hours of the morning, your body is deposited inside their camp.

Propped up, your mutilated body—arranged by the traitors—shows all the signs of a fight and heroic struggle to escape. Your body is discovered by human soldiers on morning patrol before the Kutollum can dispose of you.

The gauntlet is cast by the soldiers in the human camp. Violence rises throughout the city.

Before snowfall, the Kutollum return to their homeland...the treaty is broken.

When spring arrives, Mahan's forces break the lines in the south and march towards Castle Andilain.

The doom of the kingdom seems certain.

THE END

94. Stand And Fight

The situation is perilous. If you don't react and fast— you're likely to die.

The sargent grins his toothless grin and backs out the other end of the shop as he closes the doors.

"Take care of them, boys," is the last words you hear.

The two thugs grin at one another.

- Fight the redhead after Valda, go to page 145.
- Take on the giant brunette, go to page 144.

95. Run Deeper Into The Forest

You bolt through the trees, making sure to kick up the leaves as you go.

The thing about a Tailmain, is they believe they're smart AND invincible. They're neither. So when the beasts are trying to lure their prey into the night, what they're actually doing is showing humans right where they are.

Convenient.

Zig-zagging through the forest, you run further from the camp and the road, stopping only to make challenging grunts and snorts. The torch light stops several times, but a quick loop towards them eggs them on again.

Dorbane, you dense Kutollum, you better get those people out of there!

Unfortunately, your concern for the hostages and your friends distracts you. Tempting the soldiers wildly in a final loop to get them to pursue you, a wrong turn leads you into a small ravine.

Before you notice this, you give out another snort and growl as the torches come into sight.

… but there's no way out of the ravine.

You're trapped.

THE END

96.   Leave For Westgaiden

"This is too much for me," shutters Valda, "I don't want to stick around anymore, war or no war."

You can't say you blame her. You feel the same way.

"What about you?" you ask Dorbane.

"There are other ways to serve." With a heavy sigh, he shoulders his axe, "As for me, I'd like to find something other than the military."

"Then that makes three," you conclude. "I hear there are opportunities for those willing to venture the wild lands...and even openings for scouts."

"Anywhere but here," moans the Gypsy.

So off you venture, and for nearly a month, you work your way over to Westgaiden, the largest port in the country. You quickly find a job as guards for Jaris Ampleton, a rich spice merchant. The tasks are simple, you get to see the world from one of his many ships,...and the pay is excellent.

What more can a person want?

THE END

97. Try To Yell For Help

"This...is not good," you sigh. The drinks are really kicking in and your legs feel weak.

"I think going to our rooms would have been a better idea," shrieks Valda as the red headed man rushes her. He tries to grab her, but the lithe Gypsy side-steps, grabs one of the hammers hanging from the posts and clobbers him in the shoulder.

You hear a crunching sound upon impact.

"ARGH!" he yells, grasping the wound. "You witch!"

Valda runs around to stand behind Dorbane, who holds his axe up...swaying on unsure feet.

"Now don't go playin' boy, when ya should be workin!" reprimands the sergeant. "Come now, Burt— let the boys do their thing, willya?"

The blacksmith mutters under his breath and throws the sword he was working on, back into the coals. He throws the hammer onto the ground and marches out, openly angry.

"Oh don't be that way, Burt—the boys'll clean up after themselves this time." He turns back to your aggressors, "Won't you boys!?"

"Sir, yes sir!" they shout in unison.

"We'll feed them to the hogs when yer done, alright?" With a wave, the sargent backs out of the shop and the other set of doors slams shut.

"Helllp!" Valda yells. She looks at you, then at the devious grin of the red headed man. Her eyes widen and she breaks into a frantic. "HEELLLLLPPPP!" she screams louder.

"Ain't gonna work," chuckles the raven-top. He swings at you clumsily with his mace, taking a chunk off the stone wall of the forge. "Lots o'traitors yell when we work 'em. People don't listen no more." He gives you a snarl and swings again, this time coming closer to your face. "You'd have to start a fire to attract attention 'round here!"

Hmmm, that gives you an idea.

While Valda and Dorbane dance with the redhead, you lure the witty thug closer to the open forge. It's set low, with a diameter of at least five feet. More than a dozen strips of metal are buried in the glow of the coals. So you dance, weave and taunt until the thug finally swings like the champ he is.

The mace lands...on one of the metal strips. The blow launches fire into his face and over against the wall of the building. The thug screams, dropping the mace to grab his own flesh. This gets the attention of the red head, who turns just long enough for Dorbane to pummel him in the head with the butt of his axe.

Valda follows up by kicking the giant brunette in the groin, sending the brute stumbling backwards, flipping over the edge...and *into* the forge. To compliment her effort, you calmly pick up the mace and clobber your own foe in the back of the head. The blow sends him, unconscious...and face first...into the flames as well.

Whoops...didn't mean to do that.

Rolling in hysterical agony, the redhead leaps from the flames and crashes through the second set of doors. He only makes it a few yards before he collapses upon the ground.

Soldiers run to investigate, but you're already gone.

- Forget the military, let's get out of here! Go to page 96.
- Report the incident to the authorities. Go to page 82.

100. "Because We Heard The Call"

"So, you support our brothers from the North and from Äsä-Illäriu, being here in our lands?" Rodrick McDonnell's expression suddenly turns cold.

You start to wonder if you just said the wrong thing.

Finally he smiles again and pats you on the arm. "We all have to work together if we're going to make it through these difficult times, don't you agree?"

You smile back, "Absolutely, sir."

"Then I won't keep you further." Opening the flap to the tent, he adds, "Sign in with Sergeant Stewart, then report immediately to the army kitchen."

Valda kicks you in the backside as you walk through camp.

You spend the next seven months working in the mess hall.

The good news is...you eventually move up the chain and get to work in the stables.

THE END

101. You Decide To Head For The Hills

"There's no way we can stop this when those in charge are corrupt. They hold all the power and control." Valda kicks a stone through the trees, "We're helpless!"

It's a troubling thought, but there isn't much choice. If you go back, you'll either draw suspicion, maybe be accused and arrested. On the other hand...

"Well, if we didn't sign anything, there's no reason to stick around," shrugs Valda, "Is there? I don't intend to risk my neck for people who want to slit it."

"I agree," you reply, "let's get as far from here as we can."

Leaving the soldier uniforms and pitiful excuses for weapons, you and Valda walk into the night.

Over time, you find your place in the world, which always holds opportunities for those of good hearts and able hands. You eventually find work as rangers and take part in some well-known battles waged in the Tilliman Highlands.

...you even cross paths with the legendary Nethinim.

But that's another story altogether.

THE END

102.   You Show Up As Ordered

You show up on time and meet with six other soldiers. They all look like kids...barely old enough to enlist. After a few comments and exchanges of camaraderie, you and Valda realize that there isn't a single, seasoned soldier in the group. Even your leader, Sergeant Drier, enlisted last week and was promoted just this morning.

Your orders are simple: go meet a supply wagon and escort it back to camp.

It seems odd, to send so many men for a single wagon, but hey, you're new to the military. Your's is to do, not ask. So you march for the rest of the day until the light wanes.

You make camp for the night, very near to Cross Point.

Valda looks at you nervously.

"I have this nagging feeling we're not in a good place right now," she whispers. She sits down next to you with her rationed food.

You take a bite, eyeing the other soldiers.

Suddenly, an arrow flies through the darkness and thunks into the chest of the boy next to you! He falls over, dead.

"Get down," you shout, "We're being attacked!"

You and Valda roll behind a couple of trees, but it's too late for your fellow soldiers. Shafts whistle through the darkness, sinking into the untrained boys.

"Valda," you whisper, "can you douse the light?"

She nods and peeks around the edge of the tree. Whispering the ancient magic of her race, the camp fire fizzles out, plunging you both into darkness.

"Now what?" she hisses, "Not the brightest idea!" But she immediately shuts her mouth.

You hear approaching footsteps.

It's too dark! Closing your eyes and hold your breath. When you open them, your eyes have adjusted and you can faintly see Valda in the dim light—she's nodding in the direction of the sound.

Her own eyes are wide with panic.

Two large Andilain Soldiers are rummaging through the dead bodies.

"What about the other two that ran off?" says one.

There's a pause.

"Let 'em go," replies the other. "They're new recruits. No one's going to believe them and besides, they're not likely to have seen us anyway. We have a job to do."

You wait for them to leave...until you can no longer hear their footsteps in the distance before you dare leave your cover.

"What are we going to do?" coughs Valda, trying to get her nerves under control. "These military guys are crooked! Do you know what this means?"

"Yeah," you reply, "It means we're not safe and the men in charge back at camp are involved." You spit on the ground and then tear off your tabard. "Did you notice something today?" you ask. When she doesn't answer, you add, "We didn't sign our names to anything. Shuffle us through, no paperwork, no traces of our existence."

Valda pulls her tabard off and casts it to the ground, disgusted. She wanders through the camp, kneeling at beside each boy, closing their eyes and folding their hands across their chests.

You sigh, "Completely expendable."

- If you decide to head for the hills and leave Andilain behind you, go to page 101.
- If you decide to follow the two soldiers, go to 72.

105. "Because We Want To Serve This Land!"

"Excellent!" McDonnell grins, "That's what this country needs—true patriots, who are willing to serve for the good of the people!" He walks around the table and shakes your hand, then Valda's, though his eyes linger on her just a bit too long.

When he comes to his senses, he places an arm around each of you, turning you towards the entrance flap of the tent. "Report to Sergeant Stuart and he'll get you prepped for your first assignment."

"First assignment?" you ask, "Already??"

You hesitate and Rodrick looks at you questioningly, "Something wrong, soldier?"

"Well...*sir*, ...aren't we supposed to go through some sort of training first?" Even Valda looks thoroughly confused.

The recruiter laughs, "Nonsense! This is a time of war—we learn by DOING. We use the local strength to take care of local problems. Now report to Stewart and welcome to the elite!"

And with that, Rodrick McDonnell shoves you out into the daylight.

• Go to page 65.

106. Enlisting

The tent city is extensive, housing Evolu, Kutollum and Human armies around the grounds of Castle Andilain. Thousands of soldiers conduct training drills in the fields. Some aid the local workers in constructing stable buildings. Merchants are seen everywhere, peddling their goods.

Unfortunately, your close association now seems to be at an end.

Dorbane grips your hand firmly. "I know we talked about this and I knew it was coming...I just," he hesitates. Kutollum don't cry and your friend isn't an exception—though you see a flicker of regret in his eyes.

You feel a heavy weight in your chest.

"I know," you reply, placing your other hand over the handshake. "I have always considered you my brother, oh noble Kutollum."

Dorbane grunts, "Don't talk like that—you sound daft."

You smile, "Well, remember the plan," you add, "If the military forces create a unit mixing both Kutollum and Human's, make sure to volunteer."

He slaps your shoulder and smiles.

With many tears and desperate hugs from Valda, you leave Dorbane out front of the stables. You feel...incomplete, but...*stick to the plan*, you remind yourself.

You report to the human camp, nestled along the eastern walls of the castle.

Valda may be Iskari, but she looks human...so you both decide to keep her origins quiet.

You ask for directions from the soldiers standing guard. They promptly escort you to the camp recruiter, Rodrick.

Rodrick McDonnell.

When you enter his tent, he's eating—the table lavish with meats, fruits and bread. He's a portly man with a thick mustache and furry goatee to match. He studies you as he gulps down some wine, then wipes his mouth and tosses the cloth onto the table.

"So, you want to enlist with High King Gaston's finest, eh?"

"Yes sir," you reply happily.

"And why is that?" he ask, which throws you for just a moment.

- "Because we want to serve this land and our great king!", go to page 105.
- "Because we heard the call and want to be united with our foreign brothers, to crush the forces of Mahan!", go to page 100.

108. They Were Dressed In Uniforms

"I mean no offense," Deron laughs, "especially to you, young Dorbane, but these men were either grossly under trained, or you are far more than you appear!"

You try to ignore the indirect insult. "There were two soldiers, well trained and supplied. They had four prisoners, including your son. Two men and a girl."

"A girl?" Deron growls, "Scum harming the women folk of this land?" he grins to Dorbane and Dagan, "Lucky the bastards didn't have Kutollum women to contend with, eh?"

Both guards at the door laugh out loud, while Dorbane himself can't help but snicker. Dagan, however, holds his long face.

His father doesn't know about Aggie. You try not to smile. *Hold on, kid...hold on.*

"So you jumped into the fray and destroyed the great plans of these Evolu I suppose?"

You look at Dorbane and then at Valda. Your stomach clenches in a knot.

- "They were humans, sir." Go to page 38.
- "It was luck, that's all." Go to page 160.

109.   Follow Mountains

"I'm not willing to bet on the chance that he has a boat waiting," you grunt, "so come on! We couldn't follow him across the water anyway."

For nearly an hour, you push yourselves. The path is dry and though it's not wide, it's worn enough to provide secure footing up and around the boulders, trees and ledges. As the moons rise into the sky, you notice a section of foot prints veering off from the path.

You wouldn't have missed them altogether, if it had not been for the fact that a small stream trickles between the rocks and pools nearby.

The tracks are wet!

Someone has stepped through here...and the trail is fresh!

Valda, who loves tracking beasts almost as much as flirting with you, looks up and grins. Her dark eyes glisten in the moonlight.

"We have him!" she whispers.

- If you follow the tracks, go to page 142.
- You've been gone too long—you better get back to the camp before the wounded soldier wakes up! Go to page 130.

110. Their Tabards Sir

"It was their tabards sir," you answer. "We...assumed that they had to be from one of the armies here in Andilain. What with the situation so close to the capital."

Deron peers at you warily. "Assumed."

You can't help but feel nervous. The process did sound a lot better in your mind, before it left your lips.

You swallow. "Yes, sir."

"You know," he adds, lifting a pipe to his lips and striking a match, "those uniforms could easily be stolen."

- "But sir..." Go to page 189.
- "Isn't it worth investigating?" Go to page 158.

111. Boat Ride

"I'm not waiting," you grumble, feeling impatient. "I'll scout the shore."

You dash off into the trees before either of your companions can respond.

Creeping through the forest, you make your way along the waterline, looking for any signs of a boat.

You're in luck!

In the distance, you see a small boat tied to a tree overhanging the water. You also see someone hunched over, inspecting it.

Got you—you devil!

Kneeling down to pull your boot knife, you hear the snap of leaves behind you.

"About time you got here," you whisper.

"Yes it is," answers a deep voice.

Before you can turn around, you are hit from behind.

You awake to the sound of water all around.

You're tied up and gagged, sitting in the middle of a boat. You open your eyes in time to see Dorbane's body being pushed overboard!

You struggle and fight, but it's no use—the ropes are too tight. *Where's Valda*, your mind races. You scream, but the sound is muffled by the rag in your mouth. You look around you, panicked.

"You wonder where the girl is," says the soldier. He nods as he sits back down, "I understand." There's a peaceful expression on the scar-riddled face. "Convenient that the tools we had stashed as a back up plan, turned out to be just what I needed to dispose of three do-gooders."

He smiles as he grabs you by the throat.

You're lifted and shoved over the side of the boat...and into the cold water. The rope around your ankle is tied to a milestone.

You sink to the bottom of the lake.

You struggle for as long as you can.

The last thing you see is Valda's body anchored next to yours.

Dead eyes stare at you...wide in fear.

The last moments of her life, frozen on her face.

THE END

113.   Renegade Soldiers

"Renegade soldiers?" Captain Deron combs his long beard with his gloved fingers, considering. "That's quite an accusation from...a nobody." The words are meant to sting, but you shrug them off, unaffected.

"I'm only sharing what I believe, sir," you add without changing your tone. "My best friend here is a Kutollum," you look at Dorbane with a measure of pride, "so it...mattered to me."

Deron studies you closely. He looks to his son, but Dagan is staring at the floor. His eyes finally go to Dorbane.

"I was sorry to hear of your loss, Dorbane. The great halls will be a dimmer place without Odele McCanna."

The look of shock on your face is plain enough. *They know each other??*

Dorbane grips his axe tightly in one hand, holds it to his chest and bows low. "Thank you, Sir Erdmuth. My father ever spoke of his adventures, with you at the heart of many tales."

There is a distant look in the old Kutollum's eyes. For long moments, Deron stares into nothing...until he finally looks back to Dorbane. A hearty smile grows across his face.

"He was a great leader, your father. It was an honor to serve under his command."

What? This keeps getting better by the moment...

When he looks back to you, the expression is...more accepting. His tone, now civilized.

"How did you know these men who abducted my son were actual soldiers?"

- "Their tabards, sir." Go to page 110.
- "They were dressed in full uniforms and fought with skill, sir." Go to page 108.

115. Valda Uses Magic

"This isn't safe!" you warn her, but she isn't listening. The magic has already taken over—sending her into a mental spiral until she's forced from the experience, or it reaches its conclusion.

"Let her do her thing," says Dorbane, his eyes watching the shadow climbing into the boat.

Valda sways...then stumbles.

"She's losing it!" you bark and side-step to catch her, but she doesn't fall.

"I'm fine," she says finally, shaking her head clear.

Dorbane laughs out loud, "Well I'll be—look at that, boy!" ...and he points to the boat.

The shadow sways for a moment, then flips over the side of the vessel with a loud THUMP!

You find the soldier, snoring loudly, face first in the bottom of the boat.

Valda smirks, "I'm getting better at this."

"You most certainly are," you grin.

But the question is, what do you do with the soldier now?

- Interrogate the soldier, go to page 118
- Tie him up and take him back to Andilain, go to page 126

116. You Give Dagon His Space

You let your head tilt back and rest against the rickety sides of the wagon. The creak of the wood and the sloshing of the wine in the barrels next to you, lull you to sleep. It's been a restless night—and you find yourself dozing off.

You dream.

The great city of Andilain is on fire. The bright red and yellow lights glow across the night sky. People scream in terror as Mahan's forces destroy building after building, executing every male discovered, both old and young.

You look around, but your friends are nowhere to be found.

The three armies...the tent city itself, is gone. Not destroyed, but missing. It was never there. Nothing to defend the walls of Castle Andilain.

Trebuchet launch flaming boulders at the walls, magic fire erupting against enchanted stone.

You awake with a start, Valda's hand on your arm.

"You ok?" she asks. You nod, but you sit up quickly.

You've arrived in the tent city.

Thousands of people litter the streets, moving about quickly, like bees searching for nectar—shifting, pushing, bumping past you. Trying to get your bearings, you stumble backwards into a sheep.

Firm hands grab you. "Watch yourself my young friend," says Dorbane, "I gave my word to Dagan that we would escort him to his father." He gives the young Kuttolum a nod, "To act at witnesses that he did not abandon his post."

"Right," you add, still feeling groggy and a bit shaken by the dream, "good idea." You clear your throat. "We can escort Aggie back after that."

"That's the plan," concludes Valda.

Dagan then leads you all through the maze of tents, merchants and checkpoints, into the dwarf-district.

- Go to page 44.

118. Interrogate The Soldier

"Take that!" bellows Dorbane, "and THAT!" Each blow whips the soldiers head about...and makes the dwarf laugh louder. He cracks his knuckles and then grins at you. "I LIKE this!"

You sigh.

The soldiers eyes are nearly swollen shut—he's refused to say a word for nearly an hour.

"What are you doing with those civilians!"

A smile curls back across his face—his split lips bleeding down his chin.

He spits in your face.

"Thats' it!" cries Valda, "Let me drain his life force..."

Not even that suggestion get a rise from your prisoner.

He's a trained soldier. Older, maybe in his early forties and he's seen war. A lot of it. The scars on his face are many...and deep. Pain doesn't seem to bother him.

...so why did he run?

"I've been so stupid!" you snap. Your friends look at you curiously.

"The camp," you clarify, slapping your forehead. "That's why he ran—he wanted us to follow him—to leave the campsite!!"

"Mercy," whispers the Gypsy. "We have to get back—before the other one wakes up!"

You don't have time to react. The soldier rolls forward from where he was propped against the boat, hands free, and catches your leg behind the achilles tendon. With his shoulder, he continues to roll forward, knocking you backwards onto the ground. In an instant, he's on top of you!

The knife blade flashes in the moonlight.

...but it never falls.

The soldier grunts. His mouth opens in silence, eyes rolling back into his head—green light smoldering from both.

He falls on top of you.

"Ewww!" you yell, shoving the light, empty corpse off your chest.

Valda burps...just to freak you out.

Leaving the body on the shore of the lake, you sprint back to the camp as fast as you can.

•   Go to page 130.

120. You Abandon Your Plans

It's about time you tell Valda what's been grinding in your mind for months—ever since you left the Highlands down south.

Reaching out, you take the Gypsy's hand. She looks at you curiously, but doesn't resist.

"Valda, it's not that I want to turn my back on what's right—but where in this life are we required to save every soul we cross? When is it our time to pursue our own lives? When," you falter for a moment, "can we pursue our hearts desires?"

"That's what we're doing!" she counters, "Going to Andilain, serving the country, the king."

You shake your head. "No. That's what I've been doing because I've been too afraid to do this."

Without warning, you pull Valda into your arms and kiss her.

At first she half-heartedly struggles...but quickly wraps her arms around your neck and eagerly returns the emotions.

"Ahem."

Her salty lips are soft and...perfect.

"AHEM," Dorbane repeats, but he has the biggest smile on his face that you've ever seen. "I take it we're not going to Andilain after all? Which, I don't mind. Let others deal with their own problems this time."

Valda can't stop staring at you.

You grin at her and wrap an arm around her waist. "I actually prefer to try my hand as a merchant. To create a fortune for...my family."

You walk the hostages back to the Kings Highway and immediately set off for Westgaiden. You do try your hand at being a merchant. Dorbane becomes your partner, growing a strong exchange with his people to the North and you all become very rich. You marry Valda. You have three sons and a daughter—the pride of your life.

Even during the darkest times of war—you find a way to be happy through the love of your family. When you die, you do so of old age, leaving a dynasty to your posterity that lasts for generations.

THE END

122.   Turn Boat Around

You gently, slowly, turn the boat around.

At first it seems to be working. After a few minutes, you hear the soldier snoring.

The idiot has actually fallen asleep? Hah!

Moments later, you realize it's you that's been lulled to sleep. The rocking in the boat wasn't him shift in his sleep—it rocked because the soldier was repositioning himself.

You get hit with an oar.

Your body slowly sinks below the surface of water.

THE END

123. Talk to Dagon

You jog up between the two Kutollum.

Dagan immediately falls into silence.

You glance at Dorbane, who just grins.

"Something I said?" you ask out loud, but no one answers. "You know, Dagan, you're a lucky young man."

"Oh?" he mumbles, "...and why is that?"

You sigh, "Well, you might not know this, but those soldiers had every intention of killing that lovely girl back there and framing you for the murder."

A hand, solid as iron, grips your tunic and pulls you off balance.

"I would never harm a hair on her perfect head!" he growls. The smoldering emerald eyes burn beneath thick black brows. "They are lucky I was not free to act on my own against them..."

"Easy, son," warns Dorbane—his own hand reaching out to encourage the release of your tunic.

Dagan's face immediately softens, then shift to embarrassment. "I-I'm am sorry. I don't know what came over me."

"I do," you grin. "She is quite lovely...and I think you're a lucky dwarf, if my opinion mattered in the least."

"No. NO!" Dagan whispered, "You musn't say that! You must not anything, please! It's forbidden by my clan to find a mate outside our race—I would be banished!"

"You don't have to fear anything from me," you assure him, "But I would like to know exactly how these soldiers did get you out here into the woods...without a considerable fight."

The Kuttolum looks over his shoulder. The human men are walking slowly at the back of the party, while Valda and Aggie laugh about who knows what. The sun is climbing into the sky and a bluejay is perched on a log nearby, feasting on a grub.

"Dagan?" you prompt him.

"I've loved her since I first saw her," he starts, "Which didn't go well with my father—Captain of the Northern Guard."

You whistle, knowing how firm...even stubborn, Dorbane can be in his traditions. "I can imagine."

Dagan nods, "So we met in secret. To talk, to laugh, to take walks in the hills." He smiles brightly. "She'd listen for hours as I told tales and the folklore of my people. She'd share her dreams of running far away, to distant lands." Then he sighs, "Then we would return to...reality. We would have to pretend we knew nothing of one another."

"Painful?"

He looks at you in shock, clutching his own chest. "It kills me!"

Dorbane stifles a chuckle.

"To be a away from Aggie is nothing short of torture, I..."

"I get the point," you cut in, "So how did these soldiers capture you?"

Dagan's head lowers in shame and you notice he averts his eyes from his fellow Kutollum. "I let them."

"You what!?" snaps Dorbane, shocked.

"Let him finish, old man," you interject. "I doubt it was as simple as that...am I right, Dagan."

Dagan nods in confirmation. "I was to meet Aggie as dusk, while my fathers men were at the tavern. It was a night to celebrate with the graduating platoon, and..." He looks between you and Dorbane, "they were already there. At our secret hiding place. A knife at her alabaster throat." He grits his teeth. "That was all it took. I couldn't let her come to harm—no matter what they did to me. They had me eat a handful of root. Next thing I knew, I awoke to your Gypsy friend standing over me."

You pat him on the shoulder.

"Thank you Dagan. That's exactly what I wanted to know."

- If you talk to the humans, go to page 49.
- You decide to council with Dorbane and Valda before you reach the Kings Highway...go to page 27.

126.   Tie Him Up

"These men are not getting away with this," you growl. "This has to be stopped." You look at the heavy body. "Valda, how strong is that spell?"

She shrugs, "I'm not sure—but he shouldn't wake up for the rest of the night."

You smile, "Good. Dorbane, grab a leg—we'll drag him back."

"That's going to take some time," she adds.

"Don't wait for us," you direct, "get back to camp, tie of the other soldier and look around for any other backup transportation these men might have hiding in the shadows." You grab her arm, "And if he's awake, don't use magic. Just kill him. I don't want you to risk yourself, alright."

Without a word, she leans over, kisses your cheek and dashes off into the night.

"You really ought to marry that girl, you know," says Dorbane.

"Oh shut up and pull."

Before sunrise, the hostages have awaken, you're back at camp—and Valda has secured the other soldier. He's also still alive. Fortunate for you, there were three horses stashed in the hills, their location revealed courtesy of the young captive soldier.

Of course, Dorbane broke a few of his fingers before he felt generous with this information, but you were grateful regardless.

You escort everyone to Castle Andilain.

With Dorbane's help and that of the young Kutollum hostage, Dagan, you receive refuge in the dwarf camps. You refuse to release your prisoners until Marshall Golace from the Royal Court can be retrieved.

You explain the adventure in full, accompanied by the testimonies of the hostages. The proof is overwhelming. After the interrogation of the two soldiers, the true plot is revealed. Their leaders are exposed. Several key members of the military are charged, arrested and executed for treason—the event held for all citizens to see. The Four Kings are present during the proceedings to cement their unity in sustaining the Law.

Violence against the innocent will not be tolerated.

You are proclaimed heroes. Not only among the Human military and citizenship of Andilain, but among the Kutollum. You saved the life of Dagan, son of Deron Erdmuth, Captain of the Northern Warriors.

High King Gaston awards you, Valda and Dorbane with the Red Rose—the greatest honor the kingdom can bestow upon a civilian.

Erdmuth, as is custom, bestows you with a treasure gift from his personal estate, along with the hand of friendship. You are now, officially, known as Kääpö-Ystäv among the Kutollum...

Dwarf Friend.

You have money, fame and freedom to do anything you desire. If that wasn't enough, King Gaston grants you with a personal recommendation from his own hand.

The future is yours for the taking.

THE END

128. Talk To The Young Girl

Aggie is a pretty woman, full figured, lovely smile and golden blonde hair. A barmaid at The Three Swords—the main tavern in the tent city, she is the center of much attention. Catering to the three military forces stationed there, she had the opportunity to interact with many of the soldiers.

"Have you worked there for long?" you ask.

"Not really," she says shyly. "Only a year. My uncle, Egerton, is the steward of the tavern and when my parents passed away, he vowed to watch over me and my little brother. Toby works in the stables, caring for the officers horses. Uncle wanted to keep a closer eye on me." She blushes, "I had three proposals within the first week of our arrival—so he has me serve in the tavern with my cousins. Warns all the regulars that he'll brand them with his cattle iron if they don't keep their hands where they belong."

Her face turns red with embarrassment as she speaks.

You chuckle, "Good for him."

Aggie smiles, "He's a good man. Hates to have any of us girls work in the tavern. But, he says, the gods didn't give him boys, so he'll watch over and protect his girls in the only environment he has control over until good men can be found."

Valda bursts out laughing, "Have fun waiting."

You notice, however, that Aggie's eyes wander, if only for a moment...and rest most dotingly on the young Kutollum, Dagan.

Hmmmm, you think to yourself. "So how did you get mixed up in this?" you ask.

The barmaid flounders and flushes red again.

"Aggie?" you ask again, but she looks away.

Valda places a hand on her shoulder, "All you alright?"

"Y-yes....yes," she reassures the Gypsy. "I just, well...it was so awfully traumatic, you see."

You wink at Valda.

Both of you stare at Dagan, chatting quietly with Dorbane ahead of you.

- If you decide to talk to Dagan, go to page 123
- If you talk to the humans, go to page 49.

130. Go Back To Camp

It takes a while to find your way back to the camp, but Valda, with her rarely-erring sense of direction, leads you true.

The camp fire is out...the smoke from the wet leaves billowing into the air. The small bag of supplies are gone...as is the third soldier Valda incapacitated.

"Oh no," she gasps, then runs to the embankment.

The bodies have been rearranged.

The two human men and the young woman have been stabbed through the chest. Gunther's body has been laid near theirs, a sword shoved through his belly—so that it protrudes from his tabard.

The last victim, the Kutollum, lays nearby. He is covered in blood, but it's not his. A sword in his hand. A quick chest reveals the young dwarf is still breathing.

"They're framing him for the murders," Dorbane chokes. "The bastards are trying to frame one of my people for their *own* atrocity!"

You place a hand on his shoulder and spin the dwarf around. "No," you add, "It's not over yet."

Valda looks at you confused. You nod towards the bodies.

"You want to sign up for that? I certainly don't! Let the smarter men deal with the scum who love to kill...I say we make our fortune elsewhere."

Swallowing hard, Dorbane chokes back his anger. "And the boy?"

You give him a smile he's come to rely on. "We take him with us."

Kneeling down, you take the sword from the unconscious Kutollum and slide it into your belt. "Pull him up. We'll go to the lake and clean him up, then make for Westgaiden."

Valda nods at the bodies, "What about them?"

You look between your best friends—the only family you have. If anything happened to them, you honestly don't know if you could live with yourself. With a heavy sigh, you force a smile.

"Get him to the lake. I'll be along presently."

That night, the four of you flee to the East.

It takes you six weeks of heavy march to reach your destination, but you arrive safe and sound.

Winter comes and goes.

Though you're still looking for steady work when spring rolls around, the docks of Westgaiden have kept you sheltered and fed. Dagan Erdmuth turns out to be a fine young Kutollum and he quickly become family. Two Kutollum, a Human and a Gypsy. An odd group, to be sure...but one that soon becomes famous throughout the greatest seaport of the kingdom.

Fall whispers once more over the mountains, before you get word from the capital. The horrible murders in the kings forest still haunt the countryside.

The magistrate cannot figure out why an Andilain soldier would execute three civilians...and then commit suicide by impaling himself on his own sword.

Maybe they'll never know.

THE END

132.   You Have To Make Sure

"I want to believe you," you say in a low tone, "but you're guilty by association. I watched Gunther try to kill these people with my own eyes. You did nothing to stop him."

"What could I have done?" he complains, "Look at me!"

Dorbane snorts, "Yeah...look at him."

You glare at the Kutollum.

He shrugs, "I'm just saying."

"Then what do we do with him?" asks Valda, "We can't just let him go..."

You look around the camp. Then you look up.

"We hang him."

"WHAT!?" shrieks the youth. "I've told you what I know!!"

You shrug yourself, "So you say."

Grabbing him by the tabard, you lift him into a standing position.

"Valda, get some rope."

"PLEASE!" he begs, dropping to his knees. "Take me back...turn me in! I'll explain everything to the authorities—even admit I was a part of this! PLEASE,...don't kill me!"

His breathing quickens, sweat trickling down his brow.

Dorbane growls and raises his axe, menacingly.

• Go to page 18.

133.   Almost Catch Him!

Sliding quietly down, between the rocks, your leather clothing allows you to move silently in comparison to the soldier. In the distance, you can see the last flash of a red of a tabard moving between the trees.

He vanishes from view.

"Come on!" you moan, but it's no use. Dorbane isn't as graceful as you'd wish and he gets his muscular leg wedged uncomfortably between two boulders on the way down.

It takes nearly a minute to get him unstuck and back in pursuit.

Unfortunately, you push yourselves to no avail. You lose his trail.

He gets away.

•   Go back to Camp, go to page 130.

134. Rough Him Up

"I don't know," you say slowly. The words drop from your lips coldly, keeping your eyes fixed on him. "Valda, find me a heavy stick."

"What?" she replies, not catching on.

Dorbane, however, is already grinning.

It's just what you needed to make the kid nervous.

You smile even wider.

"Were going to break a few bones...just to make sure he's not lying."

- Break his leg, go to page 135.
- Break his arm, go to page 136.

135. Break His Leg

Valda looks around her and then hands you the tree branch used to knock out the soldier in the first place.

You heft the solid piece of wood, taking a moment to shift it around in your hands.

"L-look, we don't have to do this you know," the soldier stammers, "I-I-I don't k-know anything." His eyes pop open in sudden fear as you step forward. "WAIT! I'll tell you whatever you want!!"

"Oh," you grin, "I *know* you will." You point to his right leg and then look to the Kutollum. "Hold that leg out. I'll just take the kneecap off."

Dorbane leans down as the boy screams, "NOOO! ANYthing! I'll t-tell you anything at all!! Don't break my leg!"

Before you can swing downward, the Gypsy steps in your way.

"You know...if you break his leg, he can't get to town if you decide to let him go." She raises her eyebrows at you. "Not that I care, mind you, but I'm certainly not carrying his treacherous hide back to civilization. Are you?"

"Hmmmm," you ponder, "Didn't think of that."

- Break a few ribs—that'll get him to talk, go to page 137.
- Let Dorbane pound the truth out of him, go to page 140.

136. Break His Arm

So instead, you swing before the youth can react...and hit him in the stomach.

You knock the wind from his body, which is followed by extremely loud wheezing.

"Wow," whispers Dorbane, "nice hit. I'm surprised he didn't vomit."

"I was trying to break his arm," you whisper back.

"Oh."

After several coughs, the boy looks up, his face red and stressed.

"Please," he pleads, "don't kill me. I'm just as much of a victim as those people."

Valda spits on him, "Lair."

You pull the Gypsy back. "What's going on here? Why the hostages?"

The youth shakes his head, "I don't know the plan. I was paid to wear this outfit, to keep people from asking questions. In return, I was supposed to get enough silver to help my mother and I survive this winter on the farm."

It sounds plausible, but you don't buy it.

"Why didn't you run away?" you ask.

He smiles weakly, "I did. That's why I was sitting here, by the fire. Gunther there caught me, brought me back...and his larger buddy, Keelan, said if I moved from this spot—he'd slit my throat himself."

- If you believe him, go to page 18
- You want to believe him, but you have to make sure. Go to 134.

137.   Break A Few Ribs

"Let's see if he talks with broken ribs, then." You nod to the dwarf, "Lift his arms."

The boy squirms and screams, "No! Please!! Ask me anything you want, I'll tell! I'll TELL!"

Dorbane scoffs, "You're not much of a soldier, squealing like a woman! Where's your pride? Your honor!?"

Face pale as a ghost, tears running down his face, the boy whimpers, "But that's what I'm TELLING you...I'm *NOT* A SOLDIER!"

You have to admit—he looks completely pathetic. Even Valda is doing all she can not to laugh.

You sigh. "Fine, I won't break your ribs. Unless..."

Lowering the stick, you then point at his face —"You better tell me what I want to know!"

He gulps.

"Or we'll do THIS!" bellows Dorbane—and grabs the youths hand. Before you can react, he breaks the boys index finger at the knuckle."

From all the howling and screaming...you're pretty confident the predators of the forest will stay far away tonight.

- Slap him to shut him up! Go to page 138.
- Let Dorbane shut him up... go to page 140.

138. Slap Him To Shut Him Up

You slap him across the face so hard, it makes his head flip to his opposite shoulder.

"Shut UP!" you snap.

You feel a measure of compassion, but this is a person involved in attempted murder of Andilain civilians! It's enough to make your blood boil.

The slap doesn't get him to be completely quiet —but he does lower his tone to a whimper. He really does look pathetic.

Maybe he...doesn't know anything. He certainly can't be a soldier of High King Gaston's army. They don't recruit cowards...do they?

"What is this all about?!" you sneer, grabbing a fist full of his tabard. "*Tell me!*"

Through the tears, he sniffs, "I'm just a farmer's son. I met two men who said they'd pay me to put on a uniform and stand around." He looks at you pleadingly, "To keep people from being nosy." Shaking his head, he let's it drop to his chest. "I didn't ask any questions. Didn't care to...once they gave me so much silver. Mom and I would be fine through the winter..."

He swallows hard, "But no one told me anything about kidnapping!"

His eyes lock onto yours, his jaw locks. "I didn't agree to do THIS—but when I ran, Gunther caught me, beat me up and brought me back here. Said if I ran again, he'd stick me with the rest of them. Keelan said he'd slit my throat himself if I didn't sit by the fire and stay until he ordered me to do otherwise."

His voice trails off...eyes lingering on the bodies.

- If you believe him, go to page 18.
- You have to make sure he's telling you the truth. Go to page 132.

140. Let Drobane Pound The Truth Out Of Him

You hit the dwarf in the shoulder. "What did you do THAT for!??"

Dorbane shrugs, "Was just playing the part. No harm done."

"You broke his finger!"

"He's got nine more, what's all the fuss about?"

Valda rolls her eyes.

This is not going as planned. None of this is.

"Fine," you say reluctantly, trying to stay calm and in control, "then thrash him until he tells us what we need to know."

The Kutollum grins deviously. "THAT'S what I like to hear!!"

"WAIT!" the youth cries, "I was hired by Gunther and Keelan—the two men. The two real soldiers from Andilain!"

He looks frantically between the three of you.

"They gave me silver! I'm just a farmer—and without my dad,..." his lips tremble, "I'm just trying to take care of my mother...and they said I just had to stand around in a uniform, so people don't ask questions. It was so much money. No one said anything about kidnapping!"

He nods in the direction of the hostages. "When I heard they were gonna kill them, I ran." He looks at you, pleadingly, "As fast as I could—but Gunther there," his eyes look to the dead soldier on the ground, "caught me and brought me back. Said if I ran again, he'd kill me!"

"Liar!" screams Dorbane, bearing his teeth and raising his axe high.

- Go to page 132.

142.   Follow The Tracks

The footprints lead up through the rocks.

It's easy enough at first, to follow the wet mud, but the further the trail goes, the tracks quickly fade.

"The mud's drying out," you growl.

"We're going to lose him!" sneers Dorbane.

Hopping from rock to rock, you look for smaller signs...ANYthing to help you get back on course.

Then you hear it. The scraping of metal.

Without a word, the Gypsy is leaping ahead of you, scrambling higher onto rocks until finally, she drops down onto her belly.

"Psst!" she hisses, waving wildly at you.

Both you and Dorbane catch up and drop to a crawl.

Valda has a huge grin on her face. She points over the edge.

The soldier is slipping down the rock face. There's a small path that leads back in the direction you just came from, hidden from sight.

...a path that leads back to camp.

You start to stand up and the Gypsy grabs your arm.

"Don't," she warns. "He doesn't know we see him."

Sure enough, the soldier stops, adjusting his armor. He looks around him. After a moment, he hops down to the path and starts running full out.

"Let's take him by surprise," she adds.

- Go to page 133.

144. Take On The Giant Brunette

Without thinking, you grab the blade dumped into the flames by the blacksmith. The metal is hot, but not uncomfortably so. The tip, however, glows bright orange.

"Not so fast!" bellows the brunette soldier, lunging forward.

You spin to impale him on the hot blade, but he knocks it away with the mace. His heavy, muscular body presses close—forcing the hot blade against your own skin. In pain, you're forced to drop it onto the ground.

Valda grabs one of the blacksmith's hammers and swings at the redhead, but he dodges the blow and strikes her across the face. her hair flips around as she collapses to the dirt floor.

"Valda!" yells Dorbane, wielding his axe at the soldier.

Unfortunately for him, he's still intoxicated and one blow on the chin from the soldier, sends the dwarf sprawling to the ground....his axe flipping through the air.

It lands near your feet.

- Head-butt the soldier and slug it out, go to page 85.
- Dash for the axe. Hopefully you can get to it before the soldiers do. Go to page 93.

145.   Fight The Redhead After Valda

There is no way you are letting that scum touch a hair on Valda's head. You snatch the blacksmith tongs from the nearby post and plunge them into the forge.

You pull out a coal.

"CATCH" you yell, tossing the burning ember at the red headed soldier.

To your surprise, he turns and actually catches it.

The scream is deafening—but for some stupid reason, the man won't drop it!? Smoke billows up from his palm and he dances about erratically, bellowing like a banshee.

Even the brunette is taken back and steps away from his comrade.

Annoyed, you finally clobber the sap as he bounces your way. The metal tongs vibrate in your hands upon impact.

Unfortunately—he falls face first...into the forge.

"Grace of the White Wanderer!" shouts the brunette, dashing to aid his friend. But it's so hot, the leather armor bursts into flames and there is nothing to grab onto to pull the man out. Frantic, the soldier turns around to face you.

...and gets Dorbane's axe handle in the face.

He also falls backwards...into the fire.

"Whoops!" gasps the dwarf—and tries to pull the giant out, without luck.

"Uh, I believe it's time to run," says Valda, already sprinting to the back door.

Thankfully it wasn't locked.

- Forget the military, let's get out of here! Go to page 96.
- Report the incident to the authorities. Go to page 82.

147. Tip The Boat

You take a deep breath.

Here goes nothing.

Quickly yelling "HEY!", you tug slightly on the rim of the vessel and immediately sink under the water.

The soldier reacts, just as you supposed, rushing to look over the side of the boat.

Kicking your legs with all your might, you swim upwards, pushing on the opposite side of the vessel.

It capsizes and your enemy falls into the water.

The weight of the chain mail make it impossible for the man to stay afloat.

He sinks.

You wait.

He never comes up.

Unfortunate.

You return to shore.

"What happened?" asks Valda, concerned, "I heard you shout out there."

You shrug, "He fell in."

Dorbane grunts. "Unfortunate."

You return to camp and find the unconscious soldier gone. The prisoners, however, are alive and well.

- Go to page 53.

149.   Swim After Him

"Stop!" you warn Valda and grab her arm firmly. It takes a few shakes, but it breaks her concentration. The scowl is normally something to be worried about, but not this time. You lean in and try to get her to smile.

"Please don't put yourself at risk, Val—it would break me if something happened to you."

That did it. She backs down and silently nods.

"Besides," you grin, "I have another idea."

The water is freezing, but you're used to swimming in Binmeer Lake. This is nothing in comparison. You take a few sharp breaths and push out into the water.

Your arms stretch out, silently cutting through the water. You can see the boat in the distance. The soldier isn't rowing fast.

He thinks he's home free. Out of danger.

He has another things coming.

You breast stroke slowly as you approach—controlling your breathing. Providence must be smiling on you, because wolves howl in the distance, masking your presence.

He's relaxed...sitting back in the boat. Probably trying to figure out his next move.

It feels good to be such a thorn in his side.

You grin to yourself.

Trouble is, this is as far as your plan went.

You caught up to him, now what?

- He's a big guy...maybe you should tip the boat? Go to page 147.

- Maybe you could turn the boat around while he's resting—bring him back to shore? Go to page 122.

151. Follow The Sound Of Splashing

"Alright," grumbles the Kutollum, "I've got my wind back—let's move."

Valda checks her blade and you pull out your boot knife.

A large owl sails silently overhead, catching your attention as it blots out one of the moons for a moment. You follow its flight path as it softly caresses the stars, then vanishes from sight.

It's then you notice movement, further down the shoreline. You tap your friends on the shoulders and motion for them to follow.

Staying low and behind the trees, you can make out the silhouette of someone pushing a boat out into the water.

"He's getting away," Valda curses. "If he does, he could cause all sorts of problems for us—he's seen our faces!"

Shoving her blade back into her belt, she dashes out onto the shore.

"What are you doing?" Dorbane whispers nervously, "You'll never be able catch him in time!"

"Watch me," she retorts. Holding out a hand, she points a finger at the boat and starts singing a low-toned song. The sound rumbles deep from within her chest. The words are ancient, the tone all too familiar.

Your face goes pale.

The words. You recognize them, though you don't have clue as to what they mean.

It's an incantation to lull the soldier to sleep.

The only problem is...the last time Valda tried it, she almost killed herself!

- If you let Valda make another attempt at this unstable magic, go to page 115.
- If you stop her, go to page 149.

153. Follow The Lake

Just as you're about to race up the mountain, you hear a splash in the water.

No words are spoken,...the three of you fly down the path, towards the lake, as fast as your feet can carry you. Your heart pounds its own rhythm and your fists clench tight. All you feel is anger.

How can trusted members of the High King's army harm innocents?! Soldiers are meant to protect the people!!

The thoughts spur you on.

You reach the shore, but Valda yanks your tunic. She guides you into the trees.

"Don't expose yourself," she gasps, trying to get a breath, "we don't know where he is and he may have a bow. Let's see if we can surprise him." A moment later, Dorbane's short legs catch up and he stumbles against a tree.

"Well I'm," he huffs, "not....going out..." he gasps, "on"...he holds up a finger, then wheezes, "the water!" With a mighty sigh, Dorbane slumps down onto the ground, exhausted. "I eat fish...not swim...with them."

Valda plops down next to him.

"We can't wait!" you hiss, "He could get *away*...come on, get up!"

Dorbane frowns at you, "I know you want this dung-face, but it's wiser to go together—and if I may remind you, pup, I'm more than two hundred years OLDER than you children! A little patience please."

- If you decide to go scout the shore, go to page 111.

- If you sit and wait, go to page 151.

155. Send Valda Back To Camp

"We can't leave those innocent people alone, Valda," you blurt out, eyeing the darkness.

"I'll go back," she says.

You give her a worried look.

"Oh, don't," she adds, "I'll keep to the trees, just in case he comes back. Besides, I have to keep the skinny one in la-la land." She smirks, "It'll provide me a way to take out my hostilities."

You open to give a retort, but she sprints off.

"And you wonder why I shiver so often," mumbles Dorbane.

"Oh shut up."

You both scout the areas around, but the trail goes cold.

After an hour the trail runs cold. You're eventually forced to return to the camp...where you find the Gypsy sitting on a log, hovering over the young soldier. Hiis body lay sprawled across the ground, limp and lifeless.

She looks up and grins boldly.

"What?" she scoffs, "He's not dead. Promise."

You sigh as you shoot Dorbane a solemn look. "I think it's time we see what this guy knows. We need answers."

• Go to page 18.

156.   Lets Give Those Boys A Surprise

The blacksmiths shop is right next to the stables, which is so very convenient. You have access to more than a dozen horses...and hot objects to cause all sorts of mischief.

Pulling the horses out, you quickly make a rope halter for one of the stallions and tie several red hot branding irons to the other end. With a hoop and a shout and a whip against their rears, a stampede bursts from the confines of the barn.

Soldiers yell and dive out of the way as horses plow through the tents, dragging the irons—which light the dry cloth and miscellaneous objects on fire. In moments, the human camp is in chaos and you hear someone shouting. They've seen a human kid with a dwarf setting fire to the Captain's tent!

OOPS!

You run back to The Three Swords, grab Valda, your belongings, and immediately leave town.

It was a short stay, but an educational one.

Military life definitely isn't for you.

Let the races work out their own problems...while you work on your fortunes!

...maybe Westgaiden has opportunity for you?

THE END

158. Isn't It Worth Investigating?

"Not if it jeopardizes our alliance with the armies in these camps." Deron walks around and pats his son on the shoulder. "I do thank you, from my soul, for the return of my only son. He is young...sometimes *foolish* —but a great warrior in the making."

With that, Dagan looks up. You can tell he's quite surprised at a compliment from his own father. You wonder, for just a moment, how often Deron expresses any affection for his son at all? Dorbane rarely shows actual affection, though you know his fondness for you and Valda is deeper than words can express.

Maybe it's the way of the dwarves?

"The Dark Lords armies are marching across the world..." Deron looks at you sternly, "And we Kutollum will do our duty to King Kimmeldell the Bold...and all he calls his friends!"

The whole tend bursts out, including Dorbane, "Surum ene häbi!"

- "But sir..." Go to page 189.
- "We believe these men would have framed your son..." Go to page 188.

159. Stop And Think

Dorbane grabs you.

"Use your brain, boy. The plan's bigger than we thought! These scum aren't after my people alone—they want conflict with the Evolu as well."

You start putting the pieces together and it hits you like a kick from a mule. The humans are trying to get rid of the foreigners by framing them for crimes that will evoke the anger of Andilain's citizens. They're trying to cause a panic...a civil uprising!

"We need to get the Evolu involved," you whisper, more to yourself than anyone else."

- Go to page 24.

160. It Was Luck Thats All

"I see," smirks the Captain, "well, luck favors the brave."

You shift uncomfortably—the insults up until now make you wary of taking any credit. Better to seem humble. "We were just fortunate enough to get there before harm could be done to any of the hostages— especially Dagan, here."

"Well we won't have any more troubles from this moment forward. Dagan will be under supervision— if these rebels are seeking to gain access to me and mine, we'll watch the Evolu around the clock."

You frown. Then you look at Dorbane curiously.

"Captain," interrupts Dorbane, "these were not Evolu. The men we fought were human. They wore the red and blue tabards of Andilain."

- Go to page 38.

161. Run to Captain Deron

"What do you want now!?" the Captain yells, irritated. "I'm trying to mend the damage between our races. I already have to associate with that buffoon, Toma— must I be inflicted with your presence as well!??"

With that, the Kutollum Captain shouts orders and you're immediately thrown out of camp.

- Go to page 20.

162.   Decline The Food And Drink

"No, thank you sir," you answer, "we appreciate the offer, but we have to get Aggie back. Besides, we have to find room."

Toma nods and grins wide, "We maybe I can reward you after all! Just tell old Egerton that Toma will cover your first weeks lodgings," he winks, "food but not drink, included."

You all laugh.

The tent city, unsurprisingly, turns out to be exactly that—a sea of propped up cloth, bustling with thousands of soldiers, merchants and races from around the world. Kutollum, Humans, Evolu...even Iskari—which are blue skinned cousins to the Gypsies mix with one another. The air is ripe with sweat, meats and animal droppings, people constantly pushing and navigating their way through the streets.

You make your way to The Three Swords, one of the few solid structures in the tent city. Paid for by the rich merchants of Roland, over a hundred woodsman were employed to build the lodge in a single season. Crafted to house eight hundred soldiers within its great hall, The Three Swords caters to the needs of the racial armies, trying desperately to exist together in peace.

When you arrive, Aggie introduces you to Egerton, who happens to be the taverns steward...and her uncle. The fat old man nearly cries as the young barmaid explains the peril she experienced. Egerton expresses his gratitude by offering you a room for the first week, free of charge...on top of taking Toma's money.

"Well that was a nice surprise," chimes Valda. "We can join the military after all or take our time and look for other work if we like."

"Options are good," grunts Dorbane, "...but ale is better. I'm famished and thirsty!"

"Then you should buy the first round," you add, "and grab that sorry looking dwarf over there!"

Your friends look to see Dagan timidly scuffling near the bar, watching Aggie walk into the back with her uncle.

You laugh, "As for me, I can use a lie-down. I'm going to our room to unpack and wash this dirt from my hands and face."

"Suit yourself," scoffs the Kutollum, "I'm sure the ale will still be flowing by the time you get back."

The room is clean, but small. There are two cots and a fur skin on the floor in between. You toss the fur into the corner and throw your bag on top of it. Let them have the beds tonight, you shrug. I'm too tired to care.

- Your stomach growls fiercely. Maybe you should go get food. Go to page 185.
- You decide to sleep. Go to page 166.

164.   Enlisting As A Spy

"This is insane...AND stupid," complains Dorbane.

"I have to agree, friend," adds Dagan, "though I appreciate the noble gesture towards my people."

"Aye, as do I, but this is...well, insane...AND stupid!" repeats Dorbane.

"I'm getting the hint," you say, "but my mind's made up."

"I also think Valda will have a thing or two to say about this plan."

Oooo, the Gypsy. Yes, that could be a problem.

"But not if we don't tell her," you mutter.

"ExCUSE me? Did you suddenly fall on that soft head of yours and not tell me now?! Whadya mean, not tell her?" Dorbane looks you square in the eyes, "Do you not know how that girl fawns for you, you stupid ox?"

"Names!" you rebuke, but you have to grin about it. The Gypsies don't give their affections to just anyone. It's a magical event, a bonding. But you shake the thought from your head. Focus!

"She'll understand, because it's something I have to do," you frown, "Enough said."

"Is it now?" huffs the dwarf, "Alright then. I'll walk you to your doom of stupidity, I will. Care to assist me with this village idiot, young Dagan?"

"Aye."

You glower at them both.

Off and across town you wander, trying to think what to say to Toma to get into his good graces. Surely a good man like that would have a place for a faithful soldier like yourself!

As you approach through the stables area, you hear a great commotion in the large tent. From the flags waving above, you know this is, in fact, Toma's quarters.

An argument is raging...and there's only a hay cart standing between the three of you and knowing what all the shouting is about.

- Go to page 29.

166.   You Decided To Sleep

It's been a long and exhausting day. You can deal with tomorrow's problems...tomorrow. As soon as your head hits the folded clothes in your sac, you're out like a candle. When you wake to turn over, you see both Dorbane and Valda in their cots...the dwarf snoring like a bear.

You turn over and quickly fall back to sleep.

...what you fail to notice, however, are the two figures in the corners of the room, garbed in black.

That's unfortunate, because they slit your throat.

In the morning, the alarm is sounded throughout the city. Your bodies are found in the room, where all the furniture is over tuned and bloodied.

There was a great fight. Dorbane went crazy in the night, slitting your throat and then attacking the Gypsy. He killed her with several slashes of the axe, bleeding her out...but not before she shoved her dagger into his eye socket.

Kutollum blame the woman, the Iskari and humans blame the dwarves. The City is in an uproar...and before the week is through, fights break out between the races.

The leaders fight to keep the alliance together, but the future is unsure.

THE END

167. No Sir

"Then I think it wise for humans to mind their own business and leave us to our own." Deron's tone is polite, but sharp.

The conversation is over.

You leave the camp with both Dorbane and a somber Dagan.

"He means well," says the young Kutollum, "the men respect my father greatly."

"Don't apologize for our ways," corrects Dorbane sharply.

"No," replies Dagan, his head lowering. "No, sir."

"Well, I for one, am not allowing this to simply blow over!"

You slump against a blacksmiths wall, the echo of metal against metal, pounding out thoughts in your mind.

"It's a simple plan, you bag of donkey-dung!" growls a voice behind the wall, "We wait for Captain Deron in the alley tonight and we can frame that Kutollum bastard and get them to start a war with the Evolu!"

"Deron is a fool, but Raywhen isn't."

"Never mind you that—just do your duty and snatch that elf brat when the drugs take effect. I'll do the rest."

"Alright. Alright. We better get moving."

You grab your friends and bolt before the voices emerge from the blacksmith's shop. Dashing back to The Three Swords, you grab Valda and decide to drop in on the elf camp!

- Go to page 24.

168. Run Back Into Your Room

Ok, you think, *this is not good.*

The door rattles. You back away from it.

There's no way out, except for the window.

With no other option but to fight, you hold a blanket up to the window and break the glass with your elbow.

Climbing out onto the rooftop, you get through the opening just as the door breaks open.

"Come back here!" snarls the pitted faced man.

You give him a smile and a not-so-friendly gesture with your hand as you crawl away, out of sight.

It's a long way down and you're not quite sure how to get your feet safely on the ground. Each time you look at the street below, you stomach heaves and you have to cling to the shingles of the roof.

"There he is!" growls a voice from behind you.

Three men have crawled out onto the roof after you!

You panic and unfortunately, crawl too fast across the shingles.

Several of the wood slats give way. You can't stop sliding.

If it wasn't for your flailing about, you might have landed on the large hay stack near the stable entrance. As it happens...

You land in the middle of the street...on your head

THE END

169. I Do

"We'll," Captain Deron says impatiently, "let's hear your plan."

You've already come this far from home, experienced so much in the past few days...maybe it's time to put your courage and loyalty to the test.

"I would join the military to weed out the scoundrel's from the ranks."

Dorbane almost drops his axe.

"You...would turn traitor...for the Kutollum?" asks Deron, perplexed.

"I wouldn't consider this being a traitor, sir. I'm trying to assist in keeping the relations between the humans and your people. I would be weeding out the traitors, as far as I'm concerned."

"But those in charge might not share your definition," clarifies Dorbane. He steps forward, grabbing your arm. "Should you be caught, you could be hanged...or worse."

"Plus, there is the matter that we Kutollum would be accused of turning the humans against their own. No...I do not believe this is a wise plan."

You stand upright, at attention. "Captain Deron, with respect sir, I have made up my mind to join the noble ranks of Toma's regiment. I came to serve High King Gaston and I intend to do just that. With, or without your approval."

Deron grins at Dorbane. "Seems you keep good company after all, Dorbane. I was beginning to worry."

Your best friend hits you in the shoulder. "I think you you still should, sir."

The Captain laughs out loud and shows you out.

"Then go about your business, young human and I'll be interested in knowing what you find...if anything."

- Go to page 164.

171. Retreat To Your Room

You back up to your room and quickly bolt the door.

Great, now what?

There's a small window between the beds.

You push the cots aside as the pounding starts at the door. The thick, bubbled glass doesn't move. The window is fixed in place.

"Fairy piss," you curse.

The pounding grows, the hinges starting to give on the door.

"Knife in the chest or heights." You panic. "Crap, crap, CRAP!"

Grabbing a blanket and holding it over the glass, you strike it with an elbow. It shatters and before you change your mind, scramble out onto the roof. It's a long way down, but luckily, with the carved logs...not too hard to climb. You crawl to the corner of the building and shimmy down.

Within minutes, you're on the ground and back in the great hall. You run to Dorbane's booth.

Pushing him over, you pull the small red curtain across the opening.

Moments later, the two men scamper down the stairs and out the front doors.

"Friends of yours?" asks Dorbane.

"Wha? No. No," you answer, peering out of the curtain and sighing relief.

"Well they sure seem to know you."

You look at your friend curiously, "How could that be? I've never been to this city before...and I certainly don't know who those men are!"

Dagan leans over the table and jabs the surface with his index finger, "The small one is Corey...but we didn't hear the other one's name. They mentioned use and if we heard right, they're looking for a way to get back at you for ruining their plans."

You beam a smile to both of them, "Then let's go ruin them again."

You leave Valda laying, unconscious, on her plate.

- Go to page 33.

173. Go See Captain Deron

"But Father," Dagan pleads, "I heard them with mine own ears!"

"The only thing you're likely to be hearing is the sloshing sound of ale in your belly!" booms the Captain.

Both you and Dorbane feel it wise at this point to simply observe and speak only when spoken to. Luckily, you left the Gypsy back at the tavern—her intoxicated states usually getting the three of you into unsightly trouble with locals.

"Is this true, Dorbane?" Deron asks, "The ones who kidnapped my own son are actually here, free, and in the human camp?"

"Yes, Captain." But before the Kutollum leaders can continue, he adds, "But I must state, sir, that I do NOT know for sure that they do, indeed, work for Toma...or that the Captain has any more knowledge of these acts than you do."

"I see." Deron nods, "Thank you lad, for your candid honesty."

You feel like you're about to burst, shifting on your feet. Deron notices this.

"You have more to add, do you?"

You eagerly take a step forward, "Only that I wish to be of assistance in this matter. I realize this is unorthodox, but the people from the North Country are...well," you look to Dorbane, who only smiles, "dear to me. To think my own people are plotting against any of you boils my blood!" You catch one of the guards at the tent flap grin. "Isn't there anything we can do to assist in weeding out these vermin?"

Deron studies you for a long moment. "You...have an idea, perhaps?"

- "I do." Go to page 169.
- "No, sir." Go to page 167.

175.   Join Them For A Drink

Patrons rush past you, over to the wounded man. You almost swagger to the booth, overly proud of yourself.

Dorbane is already laughing quietly.

"Did you kick those poor boys down the stairs?" he asks with feigned concern.

"Who, me?" you ask, feigning innocence.

Dagan is swaying in his seat, intoxicated and confused.

Valda just shakes her head in disgust. "That's the public education system for you. Who knew orphanage life would, in fact, teach you something important."

"Oh?' asks the dwarf.

You grin. "Survival in close quarters."

- Go to page 40.

176. Its Time For Payback

The pain, frustration and anger swells up in you and you start to get up.

"Those dirtbags need to pay!" you hiss.

Valda kicks you in the shins so hard, you fall into your seat.

"OW!" you bellow, "What the blast was THAT for!?"

She glares at you...like the moron you are. Dorbane and Dagan, as drunk as they might be, also stare at you, dumbfounded.

The talking has gone silent in the booth next to you. Instead, you hear the moving of chairs and footsteps pass your booth.

"Wonderful," Valda hisses, "now they know we're here."

"Not the brightest reaction I've seen from you," moans Dorbane, as he peeks between the red curtains.

- If you follow the men, go to page 37.
- If you go see Captain Deron, to let him know your suspicions are confirmed, go to page 173.

177. Warning

All of you are glad you made this decision to talk with the Captain. You leave the human camp feeling full, refreshed and satisfied. You have done your duty. Dorbane laughs with Valda, teasing her about sipping wine when fine ale is available. Aggie looks content, too, though she keeps looking back, over her shoulder.

"Something wrong?" you ask her.

"I'm...not sure," she replies. You follow her line of sight, but there are so many people—the sounds of horses, clanging of blacksmiths hammers, soldiers laughing and shouting around you. The smell of leather, meats and sweat are overpowering. Sweat trickles down your brow. Your stomach turns and you suddenly feel the urge to vomit.

You stumble and collapse.

The sounds echo, drawn out...as if in a tunnel. Darkness creeps in from your peripheral vision...until everything goes black.

You wake up cold and shivering.

Blinking your eyes, you roll your head over the cool patch of ground. You hear crickets. You blink again. Stars overhead, two moons in the sky, the limbs of trees swaying over you as if concerned.

You're in a forest.

As your eyes adjust, you notice the bodies of Valda and Dorbane next to you, still unconscious.

"Good," comes a voice, "you're awake."

You sit up with a start, then regret it. Your head nearly splits open, the pounding is so loud. A moan escapes your lips as you slowly sink backward, letting your head rest in the grass and weeds.

"Yes, I'd move slowly if I were you," says the voice. A medium sized figure sits next to a small fire crackling nearby. "That's the danger of using Lakemoore Leaf. Only the most skilled alchemists can utilize the right dosage to knock you out...instead of causing your heart to stop."

The shifts to look at you, but the glow of the fire casts a shadow across his face. You can't make out any features.

"Your friends will be out a bit longer," he continues, "so we can have a short chat, before they wake. You looked like the one in charge, when talking with that moron, Toma."

You try quickly to recall who was in the tent with you, what the guards looked like, but you can't remember anything. Then you glance around. Where's Aggie?

"She's safe," the faceless figure says calmly. "She was seen by too many who know her. It was too dangerous to take her...for now. However," he says in a pointed way, "should you decide to go back to Andilain and poke your nose where it doesn't belong...well." Lifting a stick from the fire, the burning embers glowing in the night air. "Let's just say her end will be rather painful, dramatic and...exquisite."

You can't think of anything to say.

"Toma is a fool...and he doesn't know what's transpiring under his nose. You dispatched my men, which is unfortunate...but not unforeseen."

The figure stands up and takes a step closer.

"We are many and we will not be stopped. So take a hint. Your lives have been spared...this once."

THE END

179. Accept The Food And Drink

"Thank you," you say, "that would be most kind, sir."

"Oh, not at all, not at all my boy..." grins Toma.

Within minutes, cheese, cold meats and fruit are before you all, with glasses of fresh juice, water, ale and wine. None of you have to be asked twice.

You find yourself full and content.

"Well I shall deal with this matter immediately," Toma says boldly, gripping your hand firmly. "We could use good, honorable people like yourself serving these lands."

"We," you pause, looking to your friends, "...may take you up on that offer. Thank you, sir. Especially for the food."

Toma grins. "Just wish I could give you more of a reward for your efforts!"

- Go to page 177.

180. Follow The Henchmen

You slide up to the booth, slug Dorbane on the shoulder and grin, "Come ON! We got ourselves a chase!"

The Kutollum frowns at you, ale on the breath, "Huh?"

Dagan is already swaying in his seat and Valda has her head on her empty plate. She moans.

"I unpacked, came out of the room, got attacked by some thugs...and one got away!"

"Two," Dorbane slurs.

"What?"

He hold up three fingers. "TWO!" He thumbs the booth behind him, "That one that just ran out, covered in red is...what was his name, lad?"

"Corey," burps Dagan.

"Right, Corey...but the other one, I didn't get the name. Voice sounded familiar, though. He ran when he saw those two tumble down the stairs!"

You grab the dwarf and shake him, "Then you ready for some more fun?"

Valda looks up from her plate, drool, dripping over her bottom lip. "You got to hit people, didn't you? You always sound chipper when you punch a bully."

You can't stop grinning.

- Go to page 33.

181. Help Aggie Create A Distraction

For the third time, Dorbane pushes your jaw up, but it just falls open again.

Aggie giggles, overly proud of her work—but Valda isn't so sure. The Gypsy continues to tap her foot, waiting for some sort of verbal response...but nothing comes.

Dressed in a barmaids outfit, Valda looks like...a woman.

Not that you didn't know she was female before, but....woah.

"If you don't start looking at me above the neck, I'm going to carve your eyes out with my knife," she whispers. "You're *embarrassing* me!"

"Sorry!" you stammer, blinking extra hard. You had no idea there was such beauty under the dirt and boyish clothes she wore. "Sorry...It's..." a sight you won't easily get out of your brain anytime soon. You tug at your collar. *Is it just me, or did it get hot in here?*

"You alright?" Valda frowns...and Dorbane just laughs into the sleeve of his tunic.

"Uh, yeah," you reply. "No! I'm not, actually. I, uh, don't think you should go downstairs after all." You nod at her, then quickly, turn your head to look at the wall. "We don't need a distraction after all. Uh—do we, Dorbane?"

"I don't know what you're talking about, lad— that's one of the most powerful distractions I've seen in years."

"Why thank you," responds the Gypsy with a curtsy. Then pausing, "I think."

- Go to page 17.

183. Stay In The Hallway And Fight

Both men rush up the stairs...just like you hoped they would.

The narrow confines of the hallway give you an advantage—something you learned growing up in the orphanage. You shift to one wall, attacking the man with the blunt object.

He smiles...until you knee him in the groin.

Using him as a human shield, you shove him forward before the second thug can thrust his knife at you. The bigger man mows his buddy over...and they both fall down the stairs, tumbling in a ball.

There's a yell, a grunt, and the small attacker gets up, still holding the knife...but there's blood all over his hands and chest.

You quickly follow down the stairs, screaming and pointing.

"Thief! Murderer! He mugged that poor man on the stairs!!"

The small man looks around, then down at the weapon in his hand. Egerton and the patrons in the tavern turn and stare.

He runs.

- Join Dorbane, Valda and Dagan for a drink, go to page 175.
- Grab your friends and follow the henchmen. Go to page 180.

184.   You Fight Back

Bullies are nothing more than people who didn't learn manners from a good role model. Luckily, a good way to help such people understand their poor choices...*is a solid punch in the mouth.*

You hear the man's bent nose go pop as your fist make contact with his face. Oh well, it's not the mouth, but hey—it's broken and bleeding.

He doesn't, however, fall down.

Instead, a huge hammer fist swings at your head.

You dodge easily, side stepping out of the way. The first hits the wood wall of the staircase. You hear bones crack and the thug lets out a yell.

"Ooooo, that looks like that hurt!" you exclaim, mockingly.

Kicking his lead leg, the man falls forward and bangs his head into the frame as well. You raise an eyebrow.

He really IS an idiot!

Two well placed kidney blows, an elbow to the back of the head...and he's out for the count. Ready for the next fight, you take a step down the stairs.

- Stay in the hallway and fight, go to page 183.
- They have weapons, retreat to your room, go to page 171.

185. Maybe You Should Get Food

You leave the room and enter the hall.

"Going somewhere?" asks a burly man in a dirty fur vest. He blocks your path. His face is scarred...so you know someone didn't give in to his overbearing charm.

"Yeah," you answer, "a bit hungry, so if you'll excuse me?"

"No," he says...slowly smiling, "I won't."

You notice two other men, further down the stairs. They grin up at you—blocking your escape route. Even if you could get past this thug...one is trying to conceal a knife in his hand, the other taps a small wooden club against the wall as he climbs the steps.

You have to sigh for idiots like this.

"I thought you'd say that," you reply.

- If you fight back, go to page 184.
- Run back into your room and lock the door, go to page 168.

186. I Think We Should Find This Captain

Captain Deron thanks you again as you leave.

"Well THAT was uncomfortable," mumbles Valda. "I was dying to say something in there but you weren't kidding," she pokes Dorbane, "I was invisible...at best!"

"That's not how women are treated in society," says Dagan. "The military, however, is a male dominated environment. It's not that we don't believe in or trust our females. We treasure and hold our mothers and sisters very dear and precious to us. I...hope you were not offended."

You're a bit surprised when the Gypsy's expression softens and she smiles.

"Not if you put it like that," she replies. "That's...nice to hear, actually."

"Wonderful," you snort, "now that we all feel good and tingly all over, can we move on?"

Valda glares at you. You ignore her and smile over at Aggie, who has been completely silent this whole time.

"I think we should keep you with us for just one more stop, then we'll escort you home, alright?"

"Thank you," she says, but her eyes flutter for Dagan.

"I'm sorry, my friends," he says, looking away from the barmaid, "but I cannot enter the human camp. Perhaps I can meet you later, for a drink at The Three Swords?"

"Call it a date," says Valda...and one of the guards standing close by growls.

Thousands of soldiers march through the streets and alleyways. The surrounding fields are brimming with Evolu, Kutollum and Humans drilling and practicing their craft of warfare. The humans seem to be friendly with both dwarf and elf, but the two foreigners openly avoid one another.

It isn't long before you ask the right guards, and you're directed to Captain Toma's quarters.

You relate the entire tale to Toma in full, each of you testifying of what you saw and experienced.

"This is terrible!" the Captain gasps. "This will not be tolerated in any fashion," he adds, the anger in his voice swelling. "Not on *my* watch."

He's an older human, round in the middle and seemingly well respected by the men. You feel comfortable in his presence. He also treats the ladies and Dorbane with thoughtfulness and respect—having seats brought for both Aggie and Valda.

"I may have some idea's of where to start investigating." His attention seems to be drawn away and he almost mumbles to himself. "Yes, I think I know where to look first," he looks up at you, "...and who to question. You, my young friend, have done me a great service! This whole city could go up in flames if something so horrid had actually come to pass."

Looking to the ladies, he smiles compassionately, "You must be exhausted—here, let me send for drink and perhaps some food?"

- Accept the food and drink, go to page 179.
- Decline the food and drink, go to page 162.

188. We Believe These Men Framed Your Son

Silence falls in the tent.

Deron scowls at such a comment...such a bold accusation. He turns to Dorbane, ignoring you.

"Is this true?" he asks in low tones.

You watch the silent exchange between the two dwarves. Dorbane does not look at you, but you know, from experience, that he's going to have words with you later for putting him in a pickle like this.

Dorbane sighs, "It is."

The smell of bourbon pipe tobacco drifts through the air, the creaking of leather belts and boots whispering as Deron sways in place.

"...and you believe this to be true?"

Again Dorbane confirms, "I do."

The old dwarf Captain returns to the carved wooden chair behind his desk and sinks down onto the cushions. He gives you a foreboding look.

"Tell me more."

You step forward.

- "We believe the humans had a plan to murder several innocents and blame Dagan for the crime." Go to page 38.
- "They were dressed in uniforms and skilled in combat." Go to page 108.

189. But Sir.

"Do you know how sensitive and fragile this alliance is, young man?"

You close your mouth and slowly shake your head.

"Let me explain something to all of you." He lights his pipe and takes a few puffs before continuing. "The Dark Lord is on the move. Not just against my people in the North—but against your people, here. Against the Evolu across the great sea. He's attacking everyone..."

His fist strikes the table loudly, and the goblets jump. "EVERYWHERE!" he yells. "High King Gaston, most noble of your people—even though he does have elf blood in his veins, has pledged his own life to that of my glorious King, Kimmeldell the Bold. Friends they have been for many years...and now they band together to stop the darkness from sweeping across the world!"

He steps forward and pokes your tunic with the end of his pipe in the chest.

"And you want me to squabble about the doings of random thugs wearing costumes?" Deron shakes his head and laughs, "Do the Evolu think me so decrepit in the mind to fall for such a deception?"

"Buy sir," you cut in, "they were humans, not elves."

- Go to page 38.

190. Reward

Your courage, determination, honesty and integrity do not go unnoticed.

You are called to the Royal Court, where High King Gaston personally awards you and your companions with the Red Rose—the highest honor the kingdom can bestowed upon a civilian.

Once more, you are given the commission of your choice, should you choose to serve in the military. You not only saved the lives of the innocent...you proved that diplomacy and wisdom can unite the races in the face of evil.

Well done!

THE END

About the Author

Jaime Buckley is a husband, father of 11 children, grandfather, cartoonist and the creator of Wanted Hero--an epic world of adventure, magic and mystery.

Though he spends most of his time writing CHRONICLES OF A HERO or collaborating with the famous gnome historian, Höbin Luckyfeller, he does like an extra adventure when he can get it.

Jaime and all his works can be found at
WANTEDHERO.COM